KISS
Of The
NAKED
LADY
Novella

CAROL GOODNIGHT

Copyright © 2017 CAROL GOODNIGHT

All rights reserved.

ISBN: 0997152842
ISBN-13: 978-0-9971528-4-5

ACKNOWLEDGMENTS

Kelly Williamson

This book is a work of fiction. Names, characters, places and incidents either are the product of the author's imagination or are used fictitiously. Any resemblance to actual persons, living or dead, or to actual events or locales is entirely coincident

Longing

Time stood still on riven coast
Where embers prompt a blaze
In silken light of dawn's delight
Commence amidst the craze

In fevered blasts of strident wind
The souls of lovers wept
In heart's desire as one become
Despite no promise kept

Long the season heavens share
Forever yearn their fate
Sublime the memory's return
Of longing full to sate

Brood not the hours of fleeting love
Of which thee barely knew
Gain strength in yet of springs to come
Sweet splendour pray imbue

Carol Goodnight

KISS OF THE NAKED LADY

CHAPTER 1

Portofino, Italy

Two sublime seasons had passed since Carolyn Wingate pierced the razor-sharp blade of her delicately engraved snake rapier bracelet into the taut stubbled flesh of Andrew's sinewy neck.

Perhaps sublime was a bit of an overstatement, she thought. But it had certainly been satisfying to know Mike's killer was dead.

Not that she'd planned to, but she'd avenged her brother's murder. It had been a matter of self-defense.

The warm sun resting on her cheeks was a welcome relief from the gray sky that had hovered over the vineyard for the last week. Carolyn turned her delicate shoulders toward the pleasant rays.

Crimson and burnt-umber leaves loosened their hold and fell away with reluctance as the vineyard prepared to hunker down into a blissful sleep. Winter had arrived. A light breeze whirled up from the valley rustling through the withered vines to deliver the sweet woody fragrance of sun-drenched raisins, lingerers from the harvest. Bees searching for a nectar-fix hummed with monotonous insistence as they zoomed through the slender tendrils of the spring vetch cover crop. Carolyn swiped one away from her face and sighed.

Tuneful trills of the delicate red-eyed warblers congregating in the trees behind the house reminded Carolyn of Augie's grave just beyond, behind the ancient chapel.

What a kind man, she thought. *Such a wonderful friend.*

She missed him. A familiar dull ache pounded in her chest while a thin veil of tear glistened her pale blue eyes. She stared out over the vista to watch the waves, their timeless echoes dashing across the sea, racing and spraying one after the other. Ombra, her shadow, lay at her bare feet in quiet contentment.

She rarely thought of that day on the bridge in Istanbul those few months back. The day she killed Andrew. But when she did, she felt happy. Relieved. If anyone had deserved to die, it was Andrew. She reached down and scratched Ombra's large black head.

"Only you and I know the truth. Right boy?" she asked the huge dog.

Ombra licked her hand affirming their collusion.

Griff's tongue propped out of the side of his mouth in concentration. He balanced two thick slices of toast on top of the coffee cups he carried as the back screen door slammed shut behind him.

His lustrous untamed hair swirled around his head as he darted a look back in distraction. Before arriving to the table the top piece of toast fell off onto to the ground. With almost no effort, Ombra stretched his massive neck to retrieve it. He swallowed the entire piece before Griff set down the cups.

"Now I'll have to share," Griff said bending his stubbled, perturbed face toward Ombra while tearing the remaining piece of toast in half.

"Sorry darlin'."

"A little less bread won't hurt either one of us," Carolyn replied, lowering her chin to look at Griff's expanding waistline.

"We've spent enough time enjoying bread and wine. We need to get one of Augie's sons, either Augustine Jr. or Tomas, to come back here and claim their birthright. It isn't fair."

"By all means, darlin'. Let's get away from this delightful

vineyard overlooking the Ligurian coast of Italy. Let's run away to some exotic coast. Oh wait…," Griff said with a tinge of playfulness as he rolled his eyes.

"Hmm," Carolyn replied, looking back out to the sea.

"Augie loved you, Carolyn. He wanted you to have this. His sons don't want it. One is a stinking-rich plastic surgeon in Rome. The other is a renegade adventurer. They don't want it!"

"Tomas is not a renegade adventurer. He is a highly decorated member of AISE! It's the same as the CIA. The same as my brother was." Carolyn held her mouth open as if to say more, but stopped, surprised at her fierce defense of Tomas.

"Decorated, smeckorated. He doesn't want the vineyard. He's off gallivanting, who knows where?" he said as he slathered his half of toast with a generous dollop of fresh grape jelly.

Carolyn remained quiet. She knew where, or rather, why, Tomas was "off gallivanting." He was searching for Andrew. And he intended to kill him when he found him. Andrew had murdered his father while looking for her.

It was her fault Augie was dead. She looked down at Augies faithful dog and knew she'd never forgive herself. Ever.

And no matter where Andrew was, whether he was at the bottom of the Bosphorus strait being munched on by bottom feeders, or piling coal in the fiery pits of hell under Beelzebub's tutelage, she would never forgive him either.

She wasn't sure why she'd never confessed to the killing. Maybe it would feel like surrendering her victory over Andrew. She'd earned that victory, no matter who knew about it she thought, trying to reason with herself. Perhaps she felt too much the fool for falling in love with such an obvious con.

Many times she had sailed the coast alone in her yacht The Kiss Goodnight and thought about it. With the wind filling her sails, she'd slice through the waves clearing her mind of things that didn't matter. Incidental petty thoughts fell away like the flaking lead paint on the old decrepit farmhouse where she and her brother had dreamed and planned for a better life. The faster she sailed, the more toxins peeled away.

  I'll call Tomas and tell him Andrew is dead. That I killed him. It's only fair, she'd tell herself. Tomas's father is dead. He should know. But her hands would shake every time she reached for the phone. She found that it took only a moment to talk herself out of it.

  She'd keep that to herself. Unless, of course, the police found her.

  Griff need not know either.

  She'd never told Griff any of the story of her brief whirlwind romance with Andrew. That he was a gun runner pretending to fall in love with her so he could retrieve information her brother may have sent her. Did send her, in fact, in the manner of a microchip hidden in an exquisite gold and diamond ankle chain with a lovely heart-shaped clasp. Andrew had never found it, however. She hadn't known the microchip existed herself until near the end. Not finding any information, Andrew decided to kill her too, to make sure his secrets were safe. But a stab in the neck and a push over the Bosphorus Bridge had taken care of him.

  Yes, I'll keep that to myself.

CHAPTER 2

A few hours later Griff arrived back from town with the morning mail and Carolyn could see he was on edge. He fidgeted through his eggs and second piece of toast, the pity breakfast she'd prepared for him after losing half of his first one to Ombra. He scraped the eggs into a ring around the outside edge of his plate.

Finally, he set his coffee cup down with so much determination that his arm continued the movement, making a semi-circle.

"I have a great idea!" he said at last. "Let's spend the evening in that little cove where we first… you know."

With a wistful expression, he looked her square in the face and waited for her response.

Carolyn's dark ponytail fanned across her shoulder as she cocked her head. With one eye squinting in the sun she looked back at him. They'd just finished with the harvest. It'd been a hell of a task. Thank goodness the townspeople, especially Ramone from the marina, had helped them. It'd been hard work with lot to learn.

Before this harvest, Carolyn's closest experience to running a vineyard had been drinking a glass of wine at a swanky wine bar in the Midwest of the good old U.S. of A.

Griff's eyes flashed green and his entire face expressed hopefulness.

There's that glimmer. When she saw that, she knew he was bound for adventure.

"Sure, that sounds like a great idea. Let's pack a picnic."

"And a bottle of the bubbly," Griff added.

Carolyn smiled. She'd been right. He was up to something.

As she prepared sandwiches and washed apples for their picnic, Carolyn thought back. A lot had happened before she'd found herself on this pleasant hillside vineyard. The worst, of course, was the death of her brother. The sudden loss had ambushed her onto a black tide of grief where only the salve of time could hope to diminish her agonizing emptiness. It had been the most devastating thing she'd experienced in her thirty-three years of life. Well, almost thirty-four now. And that'd be saying something, even she had to admit.

She pulled the band from around her sun-tinged hair and shook her head. It failed to scatter her thoughts.

It was strange, she remembered. A vengefulness she hadn't known existed flared up inside of her that moment on the bridge when Andrew admitted killing Mike.

Dealing with the aftermath of Augie's murder and taking care of the vineyard she'd inherited from him had kept her busy. Thankfully. Otherwise, she'd have gone crazy.

But now she was at a standstill. Originally she'd thought one of Augie's sons would come back to claim the vineyard. She would happily hand it over to them. It was their heritage. Their birthright. Not hers. But they'd shown no interest in it at all.

Since Griff had arrived, he'd filled Carolyn's days with laughter and her nights with passion and romance. He finally forgave her for abandoning him on what he thought was their vagabond adventure. He never knew she'd been running for her life. He never knew the incident in the Bue Marino cave, where someone pulled her under water, was more than a prank or an accidental fall. He never knew her brother, a CIA agent, was closing in on Andrew when he was murdered.

No, Griff knew nothing about any of it. And when he held Carolyn in his arms, she liked that he saw her, not as a fearful coward that had run every time she'd faced adversity, but rather as an adventurer, a romantic, exploring the world.

Carolyn headed to the wine cellar to retrieve a few bottles of wine. She smiled as she remembered the day Griff drove up the long cypress-lined driveway for the first time. It was the day of the Cinghiale hunt.

Those damn wild boars had been destroying the vineyard all summer. One afternoon following Augie's funeral a 250 lb. wild boar charged her as she walked back from the cemetery. Ombra had come to her rescue. He'd been her shadow since that day. Before Griff arrived, it'd just been the two of them.

Ombra's bravery had earned him a deep scar along his left thigh. And apparently the Vet in town had spread the word. Augie's old friends had decided to help her make a feast of the bastards. Ramone organized the hunting party.

Griff had been the first person to arrive that day. A pleasant sigh escaped her lips thinking about it. She hadn't seen him since the night she'd crept away and sailed out alone, certain he'd betrayed her.

"What in the cornbread hell are you doing?" he'd asked as he hopped off the scooter. Carolyn smiled, remembering. She didn't get to answer him until later. He wrapped his arms around her and carried her to the couch where they resumed their passion until they heard the faint motors of the hunting party coming up the drive.

Later that evening, after all the potluck dishes were empty and meat coolers full of fresh boar, the hunting party left. Dust from the old dirt road had begun to settle and the clunkety sound of Old Man Paginelli's truck echoed up the hill as he headed down to his nearby cottage. He'd been the last to leave. The retired carabinier had nothing much else to do, so before Tomas left, he'd put him unofficially in charge of watching over her and the vineyard in case Andrew came back. She'd almost protested, but there was such an intense look Tomas's eyes when he held her hands and said goodbye.

Carolyn wasn't sure how long Griff would stay, but hoped that Old Man Paganelli would take his job less serious now that she wasn't alone. Especially since there wasn't any danger from Andrew. She felt guilty when she'd drive past his place and see him sitting on his front porch with his rifle over his knees.

Once the hillside was quiet, Griff had taken her hand and with his slow, easy stride led her back to the veranda to catch the last rays of sun. The owl on his nightly visit had flown high above them and then swooped to the lowest branch of the old oak tree that helped shade the house's southern exposure. A lavender softness had lifted from the tranquil surface of the sea to drape the close of that special day in an eerie pallor. Long shadows stretched across the hillside bathing the vineyard in a pale platinum light.

Griff pulled his chair next to Carolyn's.

"We need to talk, darlin'."

It'd been the first time he'd ever been so serious.

Carolyn remembered lowering her face, knowing he would ask her why she'd run from him. She'd begun by saying she was afraid she was falling in love with him. She'd said she'd feared he would reunite with his ex-wife and she'd used that as the reason she was afraid to get too involved. And actually, that was partially true. She'd known by the way that he'd spoken of her that a small part of his heart still loved her. Her explanation seemed to satisfy him.

He'd spent the next hour trying to convince her that after the way she'd treated him, he'd never go back to his ex-wife. After that, he'd complained for another hour about the hard time he'd had trying to find her. Carolyn had listened. She'd been thankful he'd never gotten around to asking why she left without as much as a goodbye. At that time, Carolyn had more important things to worry about than Griff and his ex-wife. Serious things. Things like murder.

But that was months ago. Between Griff, Ombra, and the hard work of the vineyard, Carolyn was able to escape her grief for longer and longer periods. Perhaps one day she would think of her brother and Augie without feeling gutted by their loss, but rather only joy they'd been in her life.

So, determined to have a good time, she helped Griff load up the old green truck with the picnic basket and blankets. Ombra hopped in back and they headed off to the marina.

"It'll be good to sail again," Griff said, smiling.

The rich, vibrant voice of Andrea Bocelli singing Christmas Carols from a few open store fronts welcomed them into the otherwise quiet city. Rumor had it that the world-renowned singer lived somewhere nearby.

Tourist season was over and the holiday season was fast approaching. They noticed a few locals finishing their lunch in the serenity of their touristless town.

After parking, they walked toward a large Christmas tree at the center of the marina. Hand-drawn pictures from the town's children decorated the tree with stick figures of their families. The mother's and dads all wore red.

"Maybe a subconscious message to the parents they'd better get into the Santa mode?" Carolyn said.

The children's drawings and the haunting sweet voice singing "What child is this" hit Carolyn's heart with a swift, unexpected blow. She opened her eyes wide to disperse the gathering tears.

Ombra, sensing something wrong, nuzzled her hand for a rub. Not happy with a quick pet, Carolyn had to get on her knee and give the dog a good scruffing before he'd let her walk on. The passionate voice continued filling the air pulling at her heart as they headed for The Kiss Goodnight.

She pursed her lips and her eyebrows hunched together.

CAROL GOODNIGHT

"Open next spring" read the sign on the thick shuttered window of her favorite shop. Stacked wooden chairs and empty flower pots barricaded the front door.

"It'll be quiet without the tourists," she said.

She'd been a tourist herself not that long ago, she thought, wondering at her sudden glum feelings.

"We should going skiing!" Griff said with the passion of a third grader. He'd noticed a fluffy black ski suit with bright red racing stripes hanging from a second-story window above one shop.

Carolyn smiled at him. Everything seemed to fascinate him. He was such a child sometimes. In a good way.

He'd suggested skiing a few times before, and she'd always shrugged it off. While the weather was temperate here on the coast, a short drive to the Alps would give them plenty of chance if they'd wanted to ski.

But Carolyn didn't want to ski. A wave of penetrating cold licked her face and poked its icy fingers into the very marrow of her bones. The air surrounding her was warm. This temperature drop, a bitter cold so frigid you could shave it with a knife, came from within. She remembered Sandy and last winter in Maine. The hair on the back of her neck stood on end as she pulled her jacket tighter.

Andrew's hired killer had shoved her friend from her Bed and Breakfast balcony to the cliff rocks below. She shivered.

"Okay. Someday," she said to Griff, remembering her mom saying the same thing when trying to postpone a no.

The sky gleamed that winter shade of blue—Purple Lace—on the Benjamin Moore paint sample swatch. Her life as a contractor seemed a million miles away. Actually, it was a little over four thousand. But that was gone, too. Along with her entire shop that burned in the mysterious fire. Andrew came to her thoughts again.

Plump, flat-bottomed clouds gathered in small groups on the horizon before they disappeared beyond the haze. The mosaic stonework echoed their footsteps on the deserted square as they headed toward the dry-docked fishing boats on the slipway. Ombra's giant black paws dragged in a click-click close behind them. Fireplaces burning pine seasoned the fresh air as it drifted over the bay.

Ombra nosed over to the stepwell where water slapped against the top step. He seemed intent on investigating a mysterious stench.

"Come on fella," Carolyn called. "Let's get in the dink."

Carolyn sat in the dinghy, but before Griff could hand her the basket and move aside for Ombra, the big dog nuzzled his leg out-of-the-way.

"Easy, boy. There's room for you," he said. "But just barely, ya big lug."

Ombra lifted his head and turned his face away from Griff. As he pivoted around trying to find his perfect spot, he stepped on Griff's foot, almost knocking him over.

"You don't watch out, I'm gonna cream yo' corn," Griff said to the dog who was now sitting in his seat next to the engine.

"Come here, darling," Carolyn called to the giant Cane Corso. "Come sit with me."

Griff looked over at Carolyn as she hung her arms around the dog's large neck. Ombra finally found the perfect spot and sat looking majestically toward The Kiss Goodnight as if waiting for his subject to squire him to his yacht.

"Gall darn polecat," Griff muttered under his breath as he rolled his eyes.

"This gorgeous polecat saved my life against a giant boar, didn't you boy?" Carolyn laughed as she nuzzled him.

The Kiss Goodnight rocked in the gentle waves, tugging at the mooring lines waiting for her next adventure. Carolyn looked at her with pride. The Kiss Goodnight was a forty-two-foot Gulet, a schooner-styled yacht made the old world way on the coast of Turkey, near Bodrum. Her graceful style, sharp bow, broad beam, and rounded aft were developed for the Mediterranean waters in Byzantiam times. A stylish slick black lower hull, trimmed by a small white line of detail separated it from the rich dark mahogany that continued topside.

Carolyn had transformed the stern into a large white cushioned lounge. A white canvas canopy above covered the area like a tent, providing much-needed shade under the burning Mediterranean sun.

"I wonder if I should rename her Eleganza, after Augie's wife," Carolyn asked Griff halfheartedly. "In honor of Augie. I never knew it was named after his wife when I changed it."

"Darlin', you know dang well Augie wanted you to name her The Kiss Goodnight. No more nonsense. Come on! Let's have some fun."

As they pulled the ropes from the mooring, Carolyn looked back at the harbor, the amphitheater of tall colorful houses, and beyond to the pine studded hillside. Then she looked at Griff. He was pretending to snarl at Ombra.

"I do love it here," she said.

Beyond the bay, the sparkling sea stretched out awaiting them. Once underway they skimmed through the crystal water and sailed past the watchful eye of the Castella Brown, a castle built on the promontory for harbor defense in the 15th century.

After rounding the peninsula, the rocks of the coastline formed its own natural fortress. The sheer cliffs rose from the turquoise sea in giant clumps of cracked clay. Silver tree leaves mingled with green pines and clung to the very top of the rock fortress appearing like a 'gangsta hat.' Tough, tipped back and ready to spurn visitors.

Carolyn leaned into the wheel as the wind wisped them alongside limestone spines that divided the steep valleys. Thrill pulsed through her as they billowed and surged, cutting a foamy path through the sea.

Except for a small fishing boat heading toward the secluded bay of San Fruttuoso, the sea gleamed empty all around. Griff stepped up behind her, gripped the wheel over her hands and kissed her cheek.

This is happiness. Finally, she thought.

CAROL GOODNIGHT

CHAPTER 3

San Fruttuoso, the ancient Abby built by monks in the 10th century rose from the secluded cove to their right. Rhythmic waves caressed the stony shores of the small hamlet nestle along the rugged coastline.

"It's quiet," Carolyn commented as they sailed by. "Not like the last time we were here."

"Nosiree! Last time divers from all over the world were diving to that anchored Christ thing. What a zoo."

"Not Christ thing, sweetheart. Statue."

"Yeah, that's what I said," Griff said as he winked.

Midway to their destination the sails flogged, and the yacht began to roll. Carolyn tried to reset the sails and change course but nothing seemed to help. She finally reefed the head sail and centered the mizzen before starting the engine. By the time they reached their bay they were ready for lunch.

Pirates bound for Genoa in the Middle Ages had named the bay Cala Dell' Oro or Golden Bay after the hidden treasure supposedly buried in the caves. Augie had brought Carolyn here often while teaching her to sail. He'd pointed out a few of the natural caves hewn by wind and rain, suggesting that they might still hold undiscovered treasure. It looked like ankle breaking terrain so she'd always passed on exploring. For Augie's sake, of course.

A faint shadow of white from deep below the surface caught

Carolyn's eye as she motored toward the narrow chasm. She flipped off the engine and hit the anchor just before passing over the ghostly white form.

"Griff, honey, check that out," she said pointing to the spot ahead of them.

"Well, kiss my go-to-hell! There's a dang boat down there. Looks new. Wonder when that happened?" he said as he looked around the forbidding rock walls.

"It's a long walk to anywhere from here, I reckon."

Ombra lumbered from his usual throne, the permanently indented spot on the lounge, to see about the commotion. He peered into the water and then moved his massive head to look Griff in the eye.

"Carolyn, your dog's lookin' at me like I'm dumber than a Louisiana stump! Make him stop."

Ombra, not amused, padded back to his spot on the cushion. He looked back at Griff with a sigh that ended in a quick snort and then propped his chin over the railing.

"You boys quit fighting." Carolyn laughed.

"Let's break out the lunch, darlin'. I'm starving. I'll get the bubbly ready," Griff said with a mischievous smile.

"Bubby? Now?" Carolyn asked.

"You know what they say about 5 o'clock, right? It's somewhere," Griff laughed. "And I proclaim that it's 5 o'clock right now in our little cove. Do you have a problem with that?" he asked her as he wrapped his arms around her in a bear hug.

The sun gleamed sterling and gold on the surrounding cliffs as gentle waves lapped the side of the yacht. The soft pleasantness of rock-clinging flowers, fresh sea water, and the warm rays of the sun wafted over them.

Carolyn moved her face toward Griff's and kissed his stubbled beard. She reached around his back and pulled him close as she nestled her face against his chest. She stood this way for a long moment breathing in the crisp, freshness of his cotton shirt.

Finally Griff broke free and disappeared into the galley. He returned a minute later with two champagne flutes. He made a theatrical production of walking to the table, uncorking the sparkling wine, and pouring two glasses half-full. He stepped over to Carolyn, nodded his head in a bow, and handed her a glass.

"Have a seat, darlin'. I have something to say."

I knew something was up, Carolyn thought as she sat back on the lounge holding her glass in the air so as not to spill it.

"I received some interesting news in the mail this morning," he began. "It seems that my uncle Bunky has passed away."

"Oh, darling, I'm so sorry to hear that?" Carolyn said. "Were you very close?"

"Not at all, darlin'. I'd only met him twice. He was my mother's brother. A bit of a black sheep in the family, if you will. He was a rock-and-roll music promoter. He used to travel with the best bands. Well, the wildest anyway. Boy, did he have the stories! He told me, the last time I saw him, that I was the only one in the family with a lick of soul. Y' know, being an artist and all."

"Kindred spirits, I see," Carolyn said.

"Yes, kindred spirits," Griff said as he stared out to sea with a thoughtful look in his eyes.

"He told me about this one time, they were surfing in Costa Rica … well, never mind about that."

He paused for a moment, apparently remembering the story.

"Anyway, old Uncle Bunky did quite well for himself. And guess which favorite nephew just inherited all of his ill-gotten gain? That would be yours truly," he said beaming and bobbing his head while waving his free hand in a motion to garner applause.

Carolyn lifted her glass for a toast.

"Congratulations sweet heart. But I'm sorry about your uncle."

Griff responded, "Why thank you my dear," he said as he clinked her glass.

"I'm not the only inheritor sittin' here," he laughed.

Carolyn put her glass to her lips to take sip.

"Not so fast, my dear. Not so fast. There's more."

With that, he bent on one knee in front of her. Carolyn looked puzzled as he took her hand.

"Now that I'm no longer a pauper, I would love for you to do me the great honor of becoming my bride. To have and hold. And hold and hold, forever and ever. And then some."

At that moment, Ombra stood up and snarled. A deep growl that morphed into low pitched bark caused Carolyn to laugh. But then she noticed the dog looking intently toward the cliff. His ears moved independently searching out sounds. He suddenly lunged forward across the lounge bellowing a string of rapid loud barks. A loud splash followed his jump into the sea. He swam toward the only rocky foothold in sight.

Griff and Carolyn looked at each other.

"Way to steal a guy's thunder!" Griff snarked. "He do this often?"

"I've *never* known him to do that. Never once heard Augie mention it either."

They watched the dog scramble to the rocky shore and stop briefly to shake his fur before bounding up the steep hillside. Griff and Carolyn stood up and watched until the dog disappeared in the brush.

"Ombra! Get back here!" Carolyn called. "I don't know what's gotten into him."

They stood watching a few moments more before Ombra came running back into view. When he got to the shore, he stopped and barked.

"He wants us to come over there," Carolyn said.

"Well, whatever HE wants…" Griff sighed.

Griff said nothing more, but stepped over to the dinghy to get it ready to launch. Within a few minutes they were looking for a place to tie up to the rocky coast. Griff steadied the boat. Carolyn jumped over to a large boulder and then scrambled up the steep climb to follow the insistent dog. He led her through a mass of bramble along the cliff wall to the shoulder-high entrance of a small cave. He then stood at the opening of the black hole and barked.

"Whaaaat?" Carolyn asked as she finally reached him.

He barked again, looking first at her and then toward the cave.

Griff finally caught up. He stood with his arm resting against the rock to catch his breath. He was about to say something when a groan came from within the cave.

Carolyn cried out, "What is it?"

She stepped back to where Griff stood against the rock.

"I think there's someone in there," Griff murmured, not altogether convinced it was a person.

"Hello. Anyone there?" he shouted.

They heard the groan again.

"I think there's someone in there," he said again. "I'm going to look."

"Be careful," Carolyn whispered.

Griff hunched over and stepped to the mouth of the cave. He called out as he entered the darkness, "Anyone here?"

"Help," a faint voice replied.

With that, Griff darted into the cave with his arms flailing in search of the source of the mysterious cry. He emerged moments later with his arms around a young man that looked to be about fifteen. He was trying, without success, to help him to his feet. The boy was dazed and blinking from sudden exposure to the light. He winced his dark eyes together allowing only a peek of sunlight through his thick black eyelashes. Just short of the mouth of the cave, he knelt down with Griff's help, and leaned against the rock wall.

"I'll go get water," Carolyn shouted on her way back down the narrow path. "Back in a flash."

She skittered down to the dink and was off. After climbing

aboard The Kiss Goodnight, she grabbed a bottle of water, and then headed back.

Griff held out his hand waving and reaching out for the bottle as she huffed back up the cliff-side. She knelt next to him and held the water to the young man's mouth. The almost lifeless boy kept his eyes closed as he ran his tongue slowly across his parched lips. His head, a tangled mop of jet-black hair, leaned against the rock in exhaustion. He wore only a pair of faded yellow shorts that hung loosely around his thin hip bones. Carolyn wondered how long he could've been here.

You can survive three days without water, she remembered. She stepped over to the mouth of the cave and bent down to peer inside. It took a few moments for her eyes to get used to the darkness before she noticed an empty water bottle laying in the soft dirt back in the darkness.

"He had water, Griff. He must have been here for days. Maybe even a week."

After a moment of rest, the young man tried to hold the bottle himself but Griff held onto it, steadying it as he swallowed. Even though he only sipped a little water, he gulped hard. The next sip went down a little easier. After the third, he leaned back to rest again.

Griff looked at Carolyn, his face drawn with concern.

"I think he must have been the one in the boat that sank."

Ombra stood watching every move.

Griff held the bottle up to the young man's mouth again. He sipped slowly. A little water dribbled down his chin and he reached up and wiped his face. Griff looked at Carolyn and smiled.

"That's a good sign. I thought he was almost gone."

When the bottle was empty Griff sat back on the rocky cliff-side.

"Is that your boat out there?" he asked.

The young man raised his hand and pointed toward the

water.

"My mother," he groaned. "She worry."

Griff leaned to help the young man to his feet. With a bit of struggle he hoisted him up and they began the arduous task of climbing down to the dinghy.

Ombra nosed in between the boy and Griff in an attempt to help.

"Carolyn, call your dog," Griff yelled.

Carolyn called Ombra just as Griff stumbled over the huge black helper. He let go of the young man and fell over into the brush. He rolled down a few feet before stopping in a thorn bush.

"Holy God Damn, Carolyn!"

"Ombra! Come here, sweetheart. Your help is not needed," Carolyn said firmly.

She took the dog by the collar and they helped each other amble down the cliff.

Griff, with his arm wrapped around the young man, tripped a few more times before they made it to the dink. Bloody and battered, but with little thought for himself, he helped the young man sit down on a rock close to the water's edge and hopped into the boat.

"Hold this steady," he commanded Carolyn as he reached around the young man and grabbed his waist. The boy more or less tumbled into the small boat on top of him. Ombra leaned over and gave the boy's face a lick, beginning at his chin and ending across his forehead. The young man let out a small sound and smiled as if he'd been tickled. Ombra then sat back near the engine and held his head high as he looked toward the yacht.

"Such a good dog, Carolyn said. You've saved a life today!"

Ombra reached his head over and licked her too.

"Glad I was here to help," Griff said while wiping the blood from his knees and elbow.

"Sorry sweetheart. You did quite well too."

After a few more bumps, Griff managed to load the young man into the Yacht. Carolyn helped settle him onto the lounge and returned with a large glass of ice water.

"Don't drink too fast," she said.

But feeling much better, the young man guzzled it down. Carolyn came back to him with another glass of water and a sandwich from their picnic. As the young man gobbled the sandwich, pieces of cheese and turkey fell around him. Ombra was very happy to help with keeping the area tidy.

"Ombra!" Carolyn shouted.

The young man shook his head before leaning to hold the big black dog around the neck.

"Thank you. You saved my life," he said. He put his face into Ombra's fur and wept.

Griff came from cleaning his wounds in time to see Ombra lick the poor weeping soul. The dog gave Griff a dismissive glance. After the boy finished both sandwiches, Carolyn asked him where he lived.

He pointed south and then curved his finger toward the left.

"He must live in San Fruttuoso," Carolyn said. "Let's go see if anyone is missing him."

She pushed the anchor button, started the motor, and then backed out of the inlet. She took a half turn on the wheel and headed south.

As they rounded into the cove of the small seaside village, they noticed a small woman sitting on the large rock promontory that guarded the bay. She sat with her shoulders hunched and her head in her hands looking down into the sea.

"My mother!" the young man shouted. "Mother. Mother. Mother!" he cried in a raspy voice.

The woman looked up as if in a daze, and then began crying, "Antonio! Antonio!"

Tears welled up in Carolyn's eyes. When she heard a stifled grunt, she looked over at Griff to see his lips pinched together in a firm straight line and his brow furrowed. She guessed it was his effort at staving off the tears gathered in his eyes, as well.

"Now aren't we a bunch...," he started to say before his voice broke. He flipped on his sunglasses and continued to hold his lips in a firm, awkward smile.

"I'll anchor. We'll need to take the dink in," Carolyn said.

Griff pulled the dink closer to the yacht. As he stepped over the ridged edge, his toe caught the outside and caused him to lumber forward and roll to his back against the hard wooden seat. He jumped up with a grunt to help the young man as he crawled over onto the dinghy, without incident.

All the while, they watched the woman on shore as she scurried back toward small horseshoe beach of the village. She kept stopping and looking as if to make sure she wasn't imagining the safe return of her son. Every time she stopped, her son would wave as vigorously as he could to reassure her that it was, indeed, him.

All the shouting and crying attracted the villagers to their open windows and doors to investigate the ruckus. They soon figured out that Antonio had been saved. A small crowd gathered as the dinghy reached the narrow stony beach. Everyone was jubilant.

Griff jumped into the shallow water and groaned. The only part of his body not already ravaged by his heroism, his feet, were met with sharp gravel. He winced with each step as he attempted to hold the boy and carry him to shore.

A horde of young men bombarded the boat to relieve Griff. They carried Antonio to his mother and set him down in a small plastic chair in the shade of one of the looming buildings that surrounded the cove. Ombra jumped out of the dink and wiggled his way through the crowd to sit next to the rescued young man. The boy wrapped his arms around Ombra and wept again.

As the crowd hushed, Antonio told them the story of what happened to him. Some of the young men looked astounded. They pointed north and shook their heads. Apparently they had all been looking for him in the very place he'd been found.

Carolyn and Griff didn't understand most of the story but at the end it was plain to see he gave the most credit for saving his life to Ombra. Everyone crowded around to pet the dog. They even tried to lift him in the air as a hero, but Ombra was having none of it. He lay limp and flat on the gravel with his head firmly planted in his paws. Then Antonio pointed toward Carolyn and Griff. Carolyn was sure she heard him say Eleganza and Augie in his excited rambling. His mother grasped Griff's hands and kissed them. She did the same to Carolyn.

A few townspeople scurried off, returning immediately with chairs for Antonio's mother, Carolyn, and Griff. Before long a shop keeper placed a platter of sausage and cheese on a small makeshift table in front of them.

Ombra stood up and stretched out his large torso before nonchalantly making his way toward the tray. Carolyn took hold of his collar, picked up a small piece of cheese, and returned to her seat. She didn't want the nice Charcuterie tray to end up as a quick treat for Ombra, even though he was the hero of the day.

After a short while, Griff reached over, touched Carolyn's arm, and glanced toward the yacht.

She nodded and stood up.

"Thank you all for this fine hospitality," she said as she walked toward Antonio's mother.

The grateful woman grasped her in a big hug-lock and sobbed again. Griff came up behind her and hugged them both. Finally, she let go. She stood looking at them with the most sincere expression Carolyn could ever recall seeing on anyone's face.

"Thank you," she said, weeping as she returned to her chair.

Carolyn, keeping hold of Ombra's collar, edged toward the dinghy as Griff shook hands all around. She was already seated when Griff, accompanied by the small crowd to the water's edge, winced his way back to the dinghy. As soon as he was aboard, she started the engine and motored back to the yacht.

Once Griff limped aboard, he seated himself on the lounge

with a huge sigh. Carolyn put her arms around him and hugged him tight.

"Yes, darling. Yes. I will have and hold you forever and ever. And then some."

***

As dusk was fast approaching, Carolyn and Griff decided to stay anchored near the tiny Fruttuoso harbor for the night. They lay silent, nestled in each other's arms listening to the soft sounds of nature. The waves rippled against the shore where a night bird called out a haunting melody in his heartfelt search of a mate. Wind whispering through the remaining leaves hushed the sound of people moving about and preparing for night on the shore.

As the sun set on the horizon, the sky darkened, and a waxing crescent moon appeared in the western sky. A pale glow on the night side of the moon reflected back from Earth. The soft, faint shadow between the horns of the crescent formed a ghostly image of the full Moon.

"That's Earthshine up there," Griff said lazily. "Leonardo Da Vinci was the first to figure it out. The old moon in the new moon's arms. It happens when light from the sun is reflected from the Earth's surface to the moon and then back to us to produce that ashen glow."

"Earthshine. I like that," Carolyn said as she kissed Griff's ear. "And I like being in your new moon arms."

As she snuggled closer to Griff and pulled the blanket over their feet, Carolyn felt a nagging sensation in the back of her mind.

She felt different. Well, she was different, she reasoned. She was engaged and going to be married. A feeling of panic suddenly washed over her. She sat up and tried to catch her breath.

"What's wrong?" Griff asked, just as they heard a splash, followed by the sound of creaking wood.

He stood at the edge of the yacht to see a small boat heading their way. When the boat got close, a weary, haggard-looking man stood up and removed his battered hat. In the beam of the boat's watch light, he placed his hat over his heart.

"My son. Antonio," he said. "Thank you."

"Oh, yes. Yes," Griff responded.

"I bring dinner. My wife. She make it," he said.

"Thank you so much," Carolyn said and started to explain how it wasn't necessary, but realized he probably wouldn't understand, anyway.

The man held up the box and as Griff reached for it the man set the box back down. He grasped Griff's hands in both of his.

"My son. Thank you."

As tears welled up in his eyes, he turned away and picked up the box again. This time he handed it up without looking at Griff. When Griff had a good hold of it, the man quickly sat back in his boat and pushed off against the yacht.

Carolyn looked after him watching his splash gleam in the moonlight until the creaking paddles disappeared into the darkness.

"Those people dodged the worst nightmare of their life today. I wonder why they didn't find him. Well, I suppose we wouldn't have either if it hadn't been for Ombra," she said.

"Yeah. Ombra." Griff laughed sarcastically while he made a show of examining his scraped elbow.

"Something in this box smells mighty darn good. And I'm mighty darn hungry, if I do say so myself," Griff said.

Carolyn opened the box and pulled out the various bowls of food while Griff went to get plates and silver. The biggest bowl contained a disc like pasta in a meaty red sauce. A thick layer of melted white cheese garnished the top. The next contained a salad of tomatoes and fresh mozzarella with a generous dose of what looked and tasted to be chopped parsley. The last box contained several large cannoli. Carolyn's favorite. She picked one up, held it in the air and took a large bite of it.

"Mmm mmm mmm!"

"Save one of those for me, darlin'," Griff said while loading his plate with pasta.

CHAPTER 4

Night slipped out with the same quiet calm as the drifting morning fog crept in. The first light carved through the weak light of dawn and began chiseling tree branches from the shrouded darkness. The ghost-gray mist buffered the waves splashing against the rugged cliff face where the Apennines Mountains cascaded into the Mediterranean.

From her vantage point, Carolyn could see people milling in and out of the blanketed hamlet. They reminded her of driftwood captured in the tide.

The sea lapped against The Kiss Goodnight enveloping the yacht with a familiar, comforting rhythm. The cool, wet vapor floated over her as thoughts of hope and happiness and of her engagement and new life filled her mind with endless possibilities. A cup of strong coffee warmed her against the damp air.

Carolyn's heart played images in her mind that tempted her to fully give herself to this moment and this feeling. She was in love. She was happy. So why do she have to try so hard to not feel skeptical?

It must be the fog. The cloak of peaceful solitude can last only so long before you begin to feel suffocated and trapped.

After finishing her coffee, she prepared the anchor and sails for the short return trip home. Home to Augie's vineyard. Her vineyard now.

CAROL GOODNIGHT

Griff and Ombra still lie quiet in the large bed below.

All the lines and canvas coated in drops of moisture from the fog made her hands damp as she readied the boat. As the sail caught the slight breeze, the yacht glided forward. Carolyn stuck her wet hands in her pockets and realized she was moving forward too. Away from her past. Away from Andrew. Away from the darkness of her childhood.

A small fluffy-tailed pine marten atop a giant boulder ballooning out of the water caught her eye. The small cat-sized creature looked at her and shook his small rounded ears. The butter-yellow winter-blooming Scotch Broom dappled like sunshine through the fog and sent a fragrant whiff on the wind. The gust filled her sails as a beam of sun broke through the haze.

The boys, awake now, were sitting on the lounge having breakfast by the time they sailed into Portofino. As Carolyn, Griff, and Ombra rode the dinghy into the harbor, they saw Ramone in the plaza hanging Christmas lights over his uncle's restaurant.

Placing his pointer and ring finger to his lips, Griff gave a loud whistle. When Ramone looked over, Griff waved both arms in the air. They hurried, making their way to him by the time he climbed down the ladder. Carolyn didn't have time to ask Griff what the big rush was. She'd been trying to keep up.

Oh, he probably wants to tell him about Ombra saving the boy, she remembered.

Ramone gave Griff a hearty handshake.

"So, Ramone. This gorgeous young woman has agreed to be my wife! What do you think about that? You're the first to know."

"Ah, Mr. Griff! Miss Carolyn! Bellissimo! I am thrilled for you," he said as he tried to hug them both at the same time.

Carolyn, a little self-conscious, realized she needed a little more time to get used to this idea before they started announcing it to the world.

I think I'd like to savor it, she thought, wondering about her hesitation.

"So, what I'd like from you, my good man, is to stay at the vineyard and keep an eye on the place. That would include taking care of this big beast," he said as he pet Ombra's head.

"Why?" Carolyn and Ramone asked in unison.

"Because, I intend to take my bride-to-be back to Charleston for a right proper wedding. We are leavin' right away. How soon can you get up there?"

Carolyn stood looking at Griff with her mouth open.

"You're gonna catch flies, darlin'," Griff said as he bent over laughing, completely tickled with himself.

"I don't know. Let me check a few things and I'll come up to see you. Probably tomorrow," Ramone responded.

"Now don't you be goin' 'round your ass to get to your elbow, son. Get up there slicker than pig snot and there'll be something extra in for you. Ya hear?" Griff said as he shook Ramone's hand again, almost off his elbow.

"Ok," Ramone answered warily.

Griff took Carolyn's hand firmly in his and walked to the truck whistling a jaunty tune. Ombra stood close to Ramone and looked after them until Carolyn turned back to call him. They both had the same look on their faces.

Carolyn's mind was blank as she stared silently out of the window listening to Griff whistle. The old green truck bounced by flaming russet fields of high grass, low scrub brush, and fragrant silver-tinged olive trees that lined the road up to the vineyard.

Small patches of blue broke up the waves of scarlet ocher pastures. Clumps of violet crocus flowers growing wild all over Italy added a touch of contrast to the landscape. The delicate purple flower has an identical, but deadly poison cousin known as the Naked Lady. Augie had cautioned her not to mistake it for the wild garlic he loved to chew while walking the vineyard.

CAROL GOODNIGHT

Her mind drifted back to their conversation.

"There's no known antidote, and once eaten not many survive the kiss of the naked lady. It's a slow, agonizing death, Carolyn. Convulsions, blood clots, and paralysis. The difference between the naked lady and the crocus is, the crocus flower has three vivid crimson stigmas, a thin tendril on one end, and a trumpet-like flute on the other. The naked lady doesn't. Come fall, I'll show you how to harvest the styles and stigma threads of the crocus. I dry them and use them to make my risotto," he'd said.

"Oh, is that your secret?" she remembered saying as they laughed.

Carolyn leaned her forehead against the window and closed her eyes.

CHAPTER 5

The sun was well over the treetops two days later when Carolyn stood at the back of the truck hugging Ombra goodbye. Ramone and Griff were heaving three heavy suitcases into the rusty truck bed. Not until that moment did she realize how much she'd come to love the vineyard and Ombra.

"I'm going to miss you, boy," she said as she knelt next to him.

The short, quick movement of fluttering wings overhead startled her. A glossy black crow glided in, swooping close to her face to alight on top of the truck. The large bird hopped on one foot and then the other, fluffing his feathers while strutting on the roof of the cab. His wings shimmered a greenish-blue as he stretched out his neck and screeched a loud caw-caw. The bird then rasped out a hoarse, grating rattle followed by a couple of clicks. His body gleamed a tinge of purple as he turned into the sun and flew away calling out another caw-caw in farewell.

The unpleasant sound of a raven was a warning from the ghost of a murdered man she'd remembered from some murky memory. The last time she'd heard it, she was certain it was a message from her brother. In fact, she'd almost convinced herself it was her brother.

CAROL GOODNIGHT

But things were wonderful now. This time it was just an old crow squawking. Just an ancient superstition, she thought as she tried to shrug off the slight feeling of doom. For a moment it reminded her of the terrible time after her brother passed away.

The truck door opened with a loud, slow creak and she slid hesitantly into the cracked-leather seat. She realized doom was a hard feeling to shake.

Ramone hopped up to sit in the back with their suitcases.

"Come on, Ombra," he said. "Let's go!"

Ombra looked toward Carolyn and then ambled, as if in slow motion, to hop up next to Ramone. She knew he sensed something.

It took close to half an hour of winding and climbing the steep rocky road before they began to descend. This morning's thoughts weaved their way through Carolyn's mind much the same as the old green truck threaded its way through the fragrant pines, palm trees, and fields of Italian ryegrass. They passed by countless rows of rock-wall fences and tiny clusters of civilization overlooking graceful coves and bays before they finally arrived in the traffic of Genoa.

Carolyn was nauseous by the time they pulled up to the Cristofer Colombo Airport's departing flights area.

It could have been the bouncy ride. But she'd had this niggling feeling before. Something was off.

"Caw-caw," reverberated from somewhere deep in her core.

Ramone and Griff had gathered the bags and were waiting at the curb. Carolyn hugged Ombra's neck saying goodbye again until the car behind them honked.

Ramone gave them each a quick hug and hopped into the driver's seat.

"Goodbye my love. I'll be back soon," she shouted to Ombra as she stepped through the airport doorway.

She'd be seeing him soon, she convinced herself as she took a last glimpse through the smudged glass.

After picking up their tickets and dropping off their luggage, Carolyn headed for the lady's room. The coffee and the bumpy ride had taken a toll on her bladder. As she turned the corner into the lavatory area, she caught the glimpse of a tall, blond man just as the men's restroom door swung shut behind him. At that same moment the scent of cedar and lemon wafted to her nose. The reaction was immediate. She froze. The tiny, thin hair on the back of her neck stood up. She felt her face grow hot. Blood rushed through her ears and the sound of roaring waves pounded in her brain.

Cedar and lemon, she thought, remembering a glass pyramid-shaped bottle of cologne on a golden tray, the only item on Andrew's perfect dresser.

"Gold, frankincense, and myrrh, the rarest and most expensive bottle of cologne in the world. A gift befitting the son of god, from an equal. From me to me," Andrew had told her.

The immediate shock stiffened her, halting her footsteps before she could take a breath.

Oh, that's crazy, she thought before taking a slow step toward the lady's room.

It couldn't be Andrew. He's dead.

But the slipstream of scent lingered. And like the deft handling of a butcher mastering dead flesh, the rancid sillage of Andrew's scent suddenly left her lonely, lost and bereft again. The pleasant fragrance which registered as rank and rotten to Carolyn's olfactory senses grew strong again as she approached the duty-free shop. On prominent display was the ostentatiously priced pyramid.

Surely no one but Andrew or his type, would buy such a ridiculously expensive cologne. The man near the restroom probably sprayed himself a free sample. She tried to smile. Maybe she should douse herself with an expensive cologne for the trip too. If for no other reason than to overpower the stench of Andrew's memory.

She smiled to herself again, this time a little more

convincingly.

After handing the flight attendant her ticket, she pointed to the front of the plane. Carolyn turned to look at Griff.

"First Class?" she asked surprised.

"A splurge for my bride-to-be. We have old Uncle Bunky to thank," Griff said with a huge smile.

The only other times she'd traveled first class was with Andrew. Not that she couldn't afford it. Her construction company had done quite well before her shop had mysteriously caught fire. She'd considered it an unnecessary extravagance. But she happily nestled in next to the window.

Griff whispered something to the stewardess and a moment later she returned with two cocktails of champagne with fresh squeezed orange juice.

Griff lifted his glass and tried to intertwine it through Carolyn's arm.

"Oh, never mind," he said as he came dangerously close to wearing the cocktail.

"Here's to shittin' in high cotton!" Griff toasted.

Carolyn clinked his glass, but sat looking at him.

Shittin' in high cotton? Wasn't that the phrase he'd used to describe his ex-wife because he'd hated her pretentious ways? Hm?

As Griff sat next to her excitedly describing all the things they would do in Charleston, Carolyn laughed. He really is like a child at Christmas.

"Here's to shittin' in high cotton!" she said with a smile as she reached over to clink his glass again.

After stopping at the Charles De Gaulle international Airport in France and the Hartsfield-Jackson Atlanta International Airport in Georgia, they finally touched down in Charleston South Carolina. It was late afternoon when they loaded their luggage into the convertible rental car and headed down Rt. 26 toward downtown.

Carolyn wasn't even sure what day it was. Were they ahead, or behind? She couldn't remember.

Griff had decided that they should take in a few days of sightseeing in the beautiful historic city before heading to Magnolia Manor, Old Uncle Bunky's estate.

After settling into their hotel across the street from Battery Park and next to the harbor, Carolyn took a shower.

"Are you sure you just don't want to order room service," she said as she came from the bathroom while drying her hair. "I'm tired and don't feel particularly well."

The room was empty.

But a note on the dressing table read: "Meet me downstairs lickity split."

"Ok then," she said to herself as she finished getting dressed. "I guess we're going out."

From the lobby, Carolyn could see Griff pacing in front of the hotel.

"Come on, darlin'. We're burnin' daylight," Griff sighed as she stepped over to him and the waiting Pedi-cab.

"Sorry, sweetheart. I'm exhausted."

Griff pulled his mouth into a straight line and then frowned while shaking his head. He reached for her hand.

Once they were seated, the Pedi-cab driver stood up and with a big push on his pedal got his bicycle moving.

They took off in the bright orange cart of the man-powered rickshaw.

"The ghosts of Stede Bonnet, the gentleman pirate, and over forty of his fellow buccaneers still linger in the Spanish moss here at White Point Garden," the driver said, pointing toward the palm lined park.

"They found their final treasure at the end of a hangman's noose in 1718. Afterward, they dangled on display from the gnarled live oaks for several days as a cautionary warning to other pirates.

Particularly Blackbeard!" he said, adding a few extra piratey sounding r's to the word gnarled.

"That period was known as the Golden Age of Piracy. Ahhh," he sighed. "Those were the days. Some of those very same trees are providing shade to tourists and park-goers. Not to mention the ghosts," he said as he turned back to them with a raised eyebrow.

"It's going to be a lovely evening," the driver said as he pointed to the Civil war cannons with stacks of mortar.

"Our guns are still trained in the direction of Charleston harbor and out toward Fort Sumter where the first shots of the Civil War were fired. Of course a cannon shot could never reach out that far."

As they rounded the tip of the peninsula, the driver slowed to a stop to let people stroll across the walkway to the seawall promenade.

"Where y'all from?" the driver asked as he turned around again.

"Here." Griff said proudly. "Just givin' my gal the tour."

"Look Griff. There's a wedding in the gazebo, Carolyn said. "Back between the trees."

Victorian gowns with fitted bodices and layers of ruffle and lace over large hoop skirts gave the ladies hourglass figures. Fans, parasols, and embroidered shawls added an extra vintage touch.

"I feel as if I've gone back in time," Carolyn said.

"Yankees." The driver laughed as he swerved the rickshaw around the horse-drawn carriage, complete with a driver in a top hat, stark white gloves, and a shiny black coat and trousers.

The driver peddled them around the tip of the peninsula, past the military hero's statues, and continued down East Battery Street.

As they drove by the meticulous restored antebellum houses, Carolyn noticed the porch ceilings all painted in the Haint blue color she'd heard about in New Orleans. Haints are the restless spirits of the dead who haven't moved on from this world into the next. They can't cross water, so they're tricked by the paint color into thinking they can't enter the residences.

By the number of aqua porch ceilings they passed, Carolyn guessed Charleston didn't much tolerate Haints.

"We'll take the ghost tour later, darlin', if you want. Plenty of ghosts in Charleston," Griff said as if reading her thoughts.

"Maybe another day, sweetheart. I'm so tired this evening."

The Pedi-cab driver arrived at the steps of the impressive United States Custom House, one of the most striking buildings in all of Charleston.

Griff got out his wallet as the driver proudly spoke of the Custom House.

"Port business is still transacted today, much as it was originally intended when it was completed in 1879. Construction of the building began in 1853 but halted in 1860 as South Carolina contemplated seceding from the Union due to the war of the Northern Aggression," he said unapologetically.

"When it began again in 1870 repair from shell damage from the Yankees was added to the construction punch-out list."

"The monumental scale of the building reflects that at one time Charleston was one of the country's busiest ports. At thirty three degrees north latitude, we are at the middle of the turning-point in the circulation pattern. The tropical easterlies, moving from east to west from sub-Sharan Africa toward the Americas brought the square riggers from Europe in the days of large sailing ships."

He continued to drone on as if his script could not end except at the end.

Griff handed the young man some cash and took Carolyn's hand.

"Thank you," Carolyn called back to the young driver who was busy counting out his tip as they rushed away.

"Let's go through the City Market on the way. There's lots of doo-dads in there you might wanna give a gander," Griff said.

Carolyn said nothing but wondered, on the way to where?

CAROL GOODNIGHT

Griff had taken on a harried kind of agitation since he'd heard the news about his inheritance and she was beginning to wonder what it was about. And how soon it would go away.

Maybe it was because she was tired and hungry, but as they wandered through the over-heated tourists lumbering past the occasional worthwhile handcraft in a sea of overpriced trinkets, Carolyn became grouchy. She didn't say anything, but she could feel it growing.

They continued walking through the stalls selling intricately woven sweet grass baskets, soaps, crafts and pottery that easily stretched two blocks long. The finally arrived at the end, to Charleston's best example of Greek Revival-style architecture, the Confederate Civil War Museum.

"If you're a Civil War nut, this place will blow your socks off. Fort Sumter uniforms, battle flags and every conceivable relic from that part of our detestable history."

"I'm not," Carolyn answered.

Not the least bit thwarted by her sullen response, Griff went on to describe how he imagined the parties.

"Imagine the dapper young soldiers and their Belles all gussied up in their colorful hoop skirts sipping sweet tea on these very steps before sending the young soldiers off to war. A last refined memory before leaving their family and friends, possibly never to return," he said. He gawked into the sky as if he were imagining the scene.

Finally he said, "It'd be hard to leave you darlin'. I'd be crazier 'n a shithouse rat if I had to go and leave you. I can tell you that."

He leaned toward Carolyn for a kiss. He could see she was tired, so he took her hand and headed across the street. They walked a little further before arriving at a plaza featuring a large fountain in the center.

"Let's stop in here for pick-me-up," he said, gazing at the sculpture in the center of the grounds.

"This sculpture represents the significance of the horse in Charleston's history," Griff said as they approached the four hulking, nine-foot bronze horses in the fountain in front of the hotel.

Significance, huh? Carolyn thought. That's not a word he's used before. Dangwangly. Possum eatin'. Butt kicken'. She associated those words with Griff.

Significance? she thought again.

"It's Quadriga. Its name is Quadriga," he repeated when he saw her confused look.

"At the top is the Carolina bird of prey. Hear tell it, they used to be pests at the market in the days when they sold mostly beef.

"Which bird?" Carolyn asked.

"Bird of prey," Griff answered.

Carolyn smiled.

"And here we are at the Grande dame of downtown Charleston," he said, with the most put-on Old South accent she'd heard from his thus far. He swept his hand toward the open door of the grand hotel. An enormous hand-blown Venetian chandelier set between two sweeping Georgian open-arm staircases greeted them into a world of southern charm and rich ambiance.

"It's twelve feet high, hand blown in Murano, Italy," Griff told her as they passed under it.

"I wonder if that's anywhere near the vineyard?" he muttered, mostly to himself.

"When Rhett told Scarlett in Gone with the Wind, 'I'm going back to Charleston where there is still a little grace and civility left in the world,' he was talking about a place like this."

Their footsteps clicked across the marble floor as they continued checking out the posh entrance.

Tucked next to the grand Italian marble lobby was an equestrian-themed cocktail and tapas lounge. The dark library paneled walls, framed thoroughbred horses, and leather couches looked inviting, as was the piano where people staying at the hotel could sit and play. Griff scanned the room and decided they would sit at the bar. After they were seated and Griff had ordered them each a pecan pie martini, he kissed Carolyn on the cheek and walked to the piano. Carolyn was surprised. He'd never mentioned that he played piano.

There was a good reason for that she found out, not a minute later, as a very bad version of chopsticks emanated through the luxurious ambiance of the lounge and lobby.

"I've always wanted to do that," he said as he returned to the bar.

"I guess it's true what they say. If you have enough money, you can be any kind of jerk you want to be. A round on the house as retribution to my audience," he said loudly as he lifted his glass. The other patrons politely looked away.

Griff laughed.

"What in the world has gotten into you?" Carolyn asked. She couldn't take her eyes away from his face. She wasn't sure she recognized him any longer.

"Money, darlin'. It's the money. I'll be all right shortly. Let me kick up a bit."

Carolyn's phone rang just then.

"Here, let me have that," Griff said. "Tonight's about us."

"But no one ever calls me, Griff. It might be important."

"It can wait," he said as he put her phone in his pocket.

"Let's pay the tab and get out of here."

"But I'm hungry! And tired!" Carolyn responded.

"I know. We're going to dinner."

When Griff paid the tab, he'd found there were no takers on his offer of free rounds. He laughed about that as they hopped into the cab.

"Snobs," he muttered.

In the cab, on the way to the next restaurant, Carolyn had had enough.

"Griff. I'm tired. I'm hungry. I'm not amused by your

shenanigans. Let's get something to eat. You can act a fool tomorrow. How much money did you inherit, anyway? Surely not enough to act like an ass," Carolyn said.

"I'm not rightly sure, darlin'. But Ole Bunk lived a mighty high-falutin life. I'm sure there's plenty enough if you want to act like an ass too," he laughed.

It was ten minutes past eight when they arrived at the restaurant. The cool atmosphere with dark walls and high beamed ceilings smelled of pepper and the rich aroma of seared meat. Carolyn's mouth watered.

In a place that had no need for a dress code, even though "jackets are required", people dressed in their finest were milling around seeing and being seen. Griff told her this was a popular hangout for Charleston's well-heeled.

Carolyn was sure she remembered that he'd spoken with disdain at the idea of the rich folk's parties and wasting money on restaurants.

Oh well, let him celebrate for a few days. As he said, he'll get over it, she thought.

"Reservation?" asked the hostess standing behind a dimly lit desk as she arched one eyebrow.

Griff pulled out his wallet, looked over his cash, and slipped her a few bills.

"Name?" she asked.

Barely audible classical music hummed over the conversation and clinking glasses of expensive wine.

From the moment they stepped into the crowded restaurant, Griff's head bobbed up and down looking around like a periscope on a submarine. He suddenly jerked back. His lips formed a thin line in a self-satisfied smile, and he rocked back on his heels. Carolyn realized he'd found his target.

She glanced around the restaurant. *What is he looking at?* she thought.

CAROL GOODNIGHT

In the back corner of the room, someone held the attention of several handsome young men in their seersucker finest. Carolyn peered around the hostess to get a better look.

Posed like a movie star dressed in old money style, but for the bleached blond hair and dangling diamonds, stood Julep.

CHAPTER 6

Carolyn didn't need an introduction to realize that the glamourous woman garnering all the attention was Griff's ex-wife. It was clear by his actions. What was also clear, was that coming to this particular place for dinner was not by happenstance.

When Julep finally noticed Griff, her face froze. But like many a bad actor, she regained her composer and resumed batting her long fake eyelashes while widening her sweet-tea smile. She rolled her neck to the side before aligning her head on a backward tilt, pushed her shoulders back, and began sauntering her swaying hips toward them in a slow, easy, side-to-side swivel.

Carolyn couldn't take her eyes away from the show. And she couldn't help but notice that Julep was leading this "Sunset Boulevard" moment with her large, overflowing breasts.

Most of the men and many of the women in the room couldn't keep their eyes off her man-melting stride either. They turned their heads in time with her slow, calculated movement. But a few, Carolyn noticed, like Griff for example, bobbed their heads up and down in the hopes of not missing anything, much like a restless boy at the county fair.

"I bet that bitch could suck-start a Harley," said a tall well-dressed man standing close to them. Griff turned his entire body toward the man and gave him the most seething glare Carolyn had ever seen on anyone. Aside from Andrew, of course. As Julep headed their way, the man made a mad dash to the back of the place and disappeared.

"Why, whatever brings you here, Griff?"

Her words flowed over him in a slow drip of condescension as she looked him up and down. She turned her shoulder against Carolyn, not addressing her at all.

"Been saving pennies for dinner, have you? I'm sure Lenny has a seat near the kitchen where you won't cause much of a spectacle." She laughed.

"Mind your manners, dear," she said as she turned to leave.

"Julep!" Griff called after her.

"I'm a wealthy man now. I've inherited Uncle Bunky's estate."

Julep turned back for a moment as if she were trying to process this new information.

With a haughty smirk and another dramatic swivel she turned and continued to walk away.

Through her hunger and exhaustion, Carolyn felt her inner kindling catch to flames. A familiar feeling raged through her, followed by an immediate and familiar action. She spun around on one foot and headed for the door.

As she stepped out into the smudgy light of the lamppost, her features succumbed to the feeling of betrayal. She sniffed back a tear and tried to keep her lips from quivering. Somewhere behind the haze of blackness the moonlight bleached a gray stillness over the street making her aware of the pounding in her head. She paused to close her eyes. She breathed deeply of the dewy night air in an effort to steel herself. Then, renewed with energy, she headed toward the corner where a glittering, garish light promised a variety of cheap carbohydrates. With each angry stride she became clearer of Griff's motivations this evening.

She was already half a block away from the restaurant when she heard the din of the fancy establishment spill out into the street as the door opened. Griff stepped out to the sidewalk and looked for her.

She was at the counter of the corner deli paying for a large bag of kettle chips by the time he caught up with her.

"What?" Griff asked while Carolyn shook her head and glared at him.

"Julep. That's what! You couldn't wait to fly back here and let her know! It's as if I don't exist! I'm tired. I'm hungry. Do you care? NO! You're only thought is to make sure that a shallow, gold digging plantation Barbie, who treated you like crap by the way, finds out you have a speck of gold!"

"It's a damn sight more than a speck," he said.

"Ugh!" Carolyn said as she pushed the door open.

"But I know what you mean, darlin'," Griff said, scurrying after her.

"I did want to come here and push it in her face! But mostly I wanted to show you off! You're the reason I went to that restaurant. To show her what a lady looks like. My lady."

Carolyn continued at a quick pace down the street.

Griff stepped up in front of her and held her arms. Carolyn stood firm and looked into his face. The breeze blew her hair softly against her cheeks and it was then that Griff noticed the dark hollows beneath her eyes. He stared into her soft blue eyes as if silently pleading his case until she finally looked away in tears.

He reached down and grasped her hand.

"Come on darlin'. It's this way. Only a few blocks back to the hotel."

As Carolyn turned around, Griff put his arm around her shoulders and held her to a stop again. Under the dim light of the historic gaslight he pulled her close.

"I'm sorry darlin'. I didn't handle that a bit right. I know I put my butt on backwards today, but I love you. I honestly do."

Carolyn looked at him.

"I'm ass backwardy today. That's all," he said as he leaned

toward her with tiny roughish smile playing around the corners of his mouth.

"I'm sorry," he whispered again as his lips softly brushed by hers.

Exhausted and not quite ready to make up, Carolyn said, "OK. Let's talk about this tomorrow."

"OK, then. Reprieve until the morrow," Griff said happily, and then with a glance toward Carolyn's stone face, he toned his expression to one more somber as they walked back to the hotel.

CHAPTER 7

> What though the radiance
> Which was once so bright
> Be now for ever taken from my sight
> Though nothing can bring back the hour
> Of splendour in the grass
>
> William Wordsworth

The next morning Carolyn spoke only a few brief words in the hour or so it took to reach Magnolia Manor. Under the circumstances they'd decided to tour Charleston another time. Well, Carolyn decided.

The silence in the car had grown past uncomfortable into a contentedness when Griff put the top down on the convertible and let the sunshine and cool, soft air blow over them. Despite being winter, Charleston was still green with only a few crisp, dried deciduous leaves scudding over the highway. Carolyn leaned her head back and raised her face to the sun.

At last they'd arrived at a crossroads and after taking a quick left turn, they noticed the two imposing iron gates marking the end of their destination. Or so Carolyn thought. Griff took her hand and kissed it as he laughed in excitement. Carolyn smiled. Despite being angry with him for his childish actions last night, she was thrilled for him.

Once they'd passed the gates, the drive to Magnolia Manor followed through the shaded woods, twisting and turning like a ribbon on the narrow gravel drive. The boughs drew close overhead to block out the pleasant sunshine.

A short way down the road, the aroma of damp leaves and rotting tree stumps, the rustle through the undergrowth, and mysterious snapping bracken caused Carolyn's mind to jump suddenly to a different time and place.

Your mind could be a clever foe, she realized as she felt the familiar stab and a film of tear skim her eyes. The odor had transported her to the woods behind her old house when she and her brother were children exploring and building rafts and forts. She took a breath. For a moment, it felt so real, so tangible.

Carolyn could remember her brother fondly now, without the agony. But sometimes a memory or thought would cut in with a fresh wound of grief as if it were creeping behind a paper-thin partition, ready and waiting for any opportunity to strike.

The low swing of a branch brushed against her arm as the labyrinth of choked wilderness encroached upon the gravel road. A sharp scratch brought her back to the present. The pointed fronds of hundreds of palmettos marching in clump formation were not present in her childhood woods. Nor were the Crepe myrtle trees that stood shedding their summer bark to expose the smooth muscled nakedness of their warm cinnamon trunks. The shredded wisps of tossed aside bark, like last year's wardrobe, intermingled with the yellow tangle of witch-hazel shrubs. The interplay of light and shadow flickered through the needle-leaf conifers on the faded flowers of the late blooming Hydrangeas as the car bounced and swerved to avoid the occasional divot in the road.

As the sky cleared ahead, the driveway followed out of the woods to the manicured grounds. Beyond the circular drive stood the manor house, grand and proud, symmetrically framed by enormous old trees draped in swaying Spanish moss.

In an effort to lighten the mood, Griff gave Carolyn the Charleston–Magnolia Manor story. He told her, without any colorful language at all, that toward the end of the 17th century a Madagascan ship captain had given a few of the residents rice seed. It had been a successful and lucrative crop and by early in the next century it had become a major export.

Magnolia Manor was strategically built on a rare plot of high ground in the tidal swamps along the Ashley River in the mid-18th century. West Indies and West African slaves built the extensive dams and dikes for the rice crops in the wet, miry soil of the cypress swamps along the river and streams of the Low Country using only primitive tools.

"Interesting," Carolyn said. "Why do they call it the Low Country?"

"Because the swamps stretch back almost one hundred and fifty miles from the sea."

"It really is spectacular, Griff," Carolyn said as she viewed the grounds.

"It is, isn't it?" he replied with a hushed tone usually reserved for reverent occasions.

The temperature hovered around sixty five degrees, pleasant and not uncommon for a winter day in South Carolina, as they strolled around the front of the large white-clapboard manor.

"I never realized… I mean, everyone knows about Bunky's mansion. He was quite the legend around Charleston. But I've never been here."

After a pause, he said, "It's magnificent! And it's mine!"

He grabbed Carolyn around the waist, leaned her back as far

as he could, and kissed her.

"Umm," she said as she regained her balance. His awe and excitement was infectious. She squeezed his hand as they headed toward the back of the house. Carolyn gasped when they turned the corner and saw the attached greenhouse.

"Oh! I've always wanted a greenhouse."

A large hanging cluster of bananas dangled from a tall banana tree inside the glass.

"And blooming gardenias! I see them!"

The rush of humid, sweet fragrance greeted her as she stepped in.

"I love it!" she said, twirling in a circle.

Griff stepped in beside her and slid his hand around her back. He pulled her tight and nuzzled her neck. His voice became husky as he whispered in her ear.

"I love you darlin'. And I'm sorry about yesterday. Very sorry."

The heady fragrance of flowering gardenia and the ambient light flickering through the banana leaves melted Carolyn's resolve to make Griff suffer a little longer for his transgression. I guess he was trying to show me off, she thought as her tongue eagerly searched for his.

"Mmm mm," He said. "We need to find the bedroom in this place."

"I'm sure there's more than one."

"Me too. Let's go find them all," he said with a wink.

Hours later Carolyn stood at the top of the sweeping bridal staircase watching as Griff headed down to retrieve their luggage from the car.

"Where's my phone, darling? I need to charge it," Carolyn shouted after him.

"In my jacket on the chair."

Carolyn smiled as her fingers lingered along the ornately

carved pineapple newel-cap on the staircase and then turned back toward the bedroom. She picked up Griff's jacket, stepped over the bedspread on the floor, and jumped on the bed where they'd just been rustling the sheets. She lay back on the pillows, plugged her phone in the charger that Griff picked up at the airport, and closed her eyes with a blissful smile.

She had so many questions. Where would they live? Would she come back to the States? Could she bring Ombra? Will he need shots? Or would Griff sell Magnolia Manor and move to Italy? But this place was so grand! Oh well, they'd think about that later. She took a deep breath and sighed.

Once her phone had charged enough to use, she hit the message button. There was only one.

"Miss Carolyn! It's Ramone!" said the frantic voice on the message.

"The vineyard. He's back. The man who killed Augie. He's back! He killed Paganelli. Shot him in the eye! Call me. I'm in the hospital."

"What the hell?" Carolyn asked, confused. She immediately redialed the phone and got a series of beeps and buzzes.

"What the hell?" she asked again. "That was thirty-six hours ago!"

"Griff!" she cried out while running to the stairs.

"Griff!" she called again as she ran down the wide staircase, two steps at a time. She threw open the door.

"Griff!"

Carolyn was next to the old well halfway across the large oval garden when she noticed the ten-year-old gray Mercedes parked up the lane.

It was the kind of car someone desperately clinging to the appearance of wealth might drive Carolyn was thinking subconsciously at the exact moment she saw the head full of bleached blond hair.

Griff, with his back to her, had his arms wrapped around the familiar blond woman.

Carolyn jerked frozen at the same time Julep stopped kissing him. She stared at Carolyn over Griff's shoulder. Her flat, vicious eyes glowered like a starving dog guarding a bone before the corners of her mouth curled up around the edges in malicious pleasure.

Time stood still. Everything stopped. Complete silence, but for the blood roaring through Carolyn's brain.

When time began to move again, it had slowed to a crawl.

Griff turned his head to look at Carolyn, his arms still wrapped around Julep's hips. Julep's smirk grew wider now that she was sure Carolyn had noticed them. Carolyn, caught in mid-step, reached her hand out to the well for balance so as not to stumble to the ground. Her legs trembled.

The surprise and look of guilt on Griff's face told her that her engagement was over. Just like that. No long, agonizing discussions. No wondering if it would work out. No stopping to ponder which way to go or ask directions. This road was closed.

Has he lied to me all along? she wondered as she stood still while the world spun around her in slow motion.

An explosive report cracked her attention deeper into the mental fog.

The rifle shot at my brother's funeral?

She looked up into the sun.

No, it wasn't that day. It wasn't ungodly hot. There were no uniforms. No shiny medals burning holes into her heart. It's pleasant. The birds are singing and the silver moss continued its lazy dance in the gentle breeze.

Crack! She heard the sound again. Seconds later she saw Griff jerk. Julep bent to him as he fell to the ground. Another crack hit the tail light of her old Mercedes.

Julep's smirk did a quick morph into something more akin to a Chelsea grin, the Joker's smile, before she dived into the open door of her car. Seconds later the engine gunned, and she disappeared in a cloud of dust.

Carolyn stood there. It was a dream. It must be. She heard another crack… and then a whir as searing heat pierced her arm. The force pushed her over the side of the well. She reached out as she tumbled forward. One of her arms was not cooperating.

She tumbled over and over again, banging her head on the well walls like a tennis shoe in the dryer. As she plummeted and bounced, a thought caught hold of her. Ramone's message. She'd only heard it a moment ago but it seemed like another lifetime. She couldn't even allow herself the possibility to think it. Or could she?

Andrew?

Splash.

The cold, wet welcome at the bottom of the well jolted her back to the here and now.

With her good arm she reached the side wall and managed a finger hold between the rock wall crevices. Her feet dangled, not touching bottom as she floated in the chilly water.

Another crack brought her further back into reality. She caught her breath and held still. She stared at her fingers holding the rocky edge while her feet skimmed through the water looking for a foothold.

A shadowy outline flickered at the top of the well. Carolyn looked up with dread. Like a street lamp in a horror movie, Andrew's pale, stiff hair glinted in the light. Sheer terror ascended the murky depths of the well and crawled down to greet her.

"My dear. I can't begin to tell you how it pleases me to see you again. Especially like this. A snail in a muck hole. A slimy hanger-on. Pity I have no salt." He laughed.

"Any final words before you meet your brother?" Andrew asked.

"I thought not," he said as his shadow covered the well.

Carolyn pushed back and sank down as far as she could.

CAROL GOODNIGHT

Psew!

A bullet whizzed toward her. The deafening blast from the shot reverberated around the well, roaring in her ears, before the sound settled into a constant buzz. The well disappeared around her to become a wet, black splotch. Beyond the continuing dull drone of the gunshot was only deathly silence.

A second bullet whizzed through the well and hit her in the same arm that'd already been hit. She jerked before going limp, and then floated to the top with her face submerged. She waited for the next shot.

Her mind willed itself back to The Kiss Goodnight. She lay on the lounge in the setting sun and watched the gannets play far out from shore. Between the patchy network of clouds, the sky burned pink and orange letting the blue drift off into the atmosphere. The magnificent deception brought her calm and peace. She floated. She gave herself over to it. The hollow echo at the center of her soul began a warm hum, and the darkness beckoned her into an unknown void. The pleasure of anticipation smoldered through her.

CAW! CAW! CAW!

As if a mysterious harbinger of an imprisoned spirit, a large black crow perched at the top of the well. He sounded his blaring alarm, set to full-on volcanic hatred. The loud, hoarse noise pulled Carolyn from the warm softness where she'd been floating to the cold, dark, watery hole where she found herself, once again, engulfed in chilling blackness.

Desperate for oxygen, she took in agonizing slow breaths while trying not to move. In... out... in... out.

She listened. Only the faint, dank sound of dripping moisture seeping through the jagged uneven stones lining the narrow hell could be heard above the constant ringing in her ears. The smell penetrated her lungs and formed the taste of stale fungus on her lips. She held her face just above the surface hoping to appear dead. Every beat of her heart gushed through her arm with the intenseness of a banging ball-peen hammer.

In the long cold hours of hanging in that dark, wicked place something changed in Carolyn. The macabre and sinister faces of gargoyles, ghouls and zombies lurked and clawed at her edges waiting to prey. At some point the shadowy, nefarious realm began to mesmerize her and a unique thought took form. A murderous thought - with a distinct undertone of mold.

A scratching sound, like rats caught in a stone trap, whispered through the well only adding to its evil essence. She wasn't sure how long she'd floated... listening, changing and absorbing, but when she dared to look up, she saw the night sky from the entrance of her private underworld... Her birthplace. The place where darkness had swallowed her and an evilness now permeated her reborn self. It had taken over completely and was residing quite comfortably by the time she started climbing.

Gripping the tiny crevices between the crumbling mortar pierced the skin on her fingers and toes causing them to bleed. The slimy walls became all the more slippery. Her right arm was useless except for the biting sharp-toothed pain that served to stoke her rage.

She reached to the next fingerhold and rested.

Balance, find a toe-hold, and push!

Every muscle in her body ached as she repeated this for hours. The cold and pain felt oddly outside of her, as if it were a dream or a movie where she watched someone else suffer.

The width of the well was the length of her legs and when she grew too exhausted to move, she positioned her back against the side and pushed against the opposite wall with her feet. The uneven cold rocks dug into her spine. They gouged and seared, shaping the evil thing within her. Instead of feeling it as pain, it had become a welcome forge.

A few remaining stars filtered through the strands of gray light above. Somewhere far off, the old wooden bones of goliath oaks creaked as they stretched their unwieldy arms.

Darkness finally gave way to a light, hazy swirl in the sky.

CAROL GOODNIGHT

Two bright-yellow parallel-stripes on a rounded, oval hump strobed in and out of her focus. Long brownish jerking legs, or were they arms she wondered, extended forward grasping into space. Carolyn slapped the giant spider and watched as it drifted down into the dark hole, wafting back and forth on its finely spun zigzag web.

"Better you than me, pal," she said with an unfamiliar laugh.

When she reached the top of the well, the muffled sound of birds flitting through leaves in the brown-curl of death welcomed her back to life. Hesitating in trepidation, she wondered if Andrew was still there, waiting. Pulling on her resolve, she straddled the wall before rolling over the top to land in the neat circle of pine-needle mulch.

A light, cold wind blew across the manicured grounds carrying with it the last trace of the desperate night. Long black shadows stretched from the manor house, clinging across the lawn to impart a sense of doom. As the sun edged over the trees to the east, Carolyn lifted her face to its warmth. The welcome, fresh scent of conifer needles filled her nose. As she could barely move anyway, she took a thankful breath, closed her eyes, and lay motionless next to the well.

***

The sun was high in the sky when Carolyn felt the faint tickle on her eyelid. It took a minute to focus on the little Lhasa Apso licking her.

Have I missed a day? she wondered. *How long have I been out?*

Her muscles screamed when she tried to move. She groaned as she lifted to her knees and peered around. She immediately hunched back down. She saw a man approaching and could just barely hear him speaking.

"Yes, at old Bunky's place. Out here on the Ashley river. Yes. I'm the caretaker. Yes. I'll wait. Lily! You get back here, you stubborn old girl. Lily!"

The dog barked at Carolyn.

"Go away!" she whispered. "Get out of here!"

Lily's barking drew the caretaker to the well. Carolyn's first thought was to run, but she could barely move.

As the caretaker rounded the well, the first thing she noticed about him was his head full of white hair glinting in the sun and for a moment she was reminded of Augie.

"Whoa, Whoa. What's going on? What happened here? Who are you?" the caretaker asked as he reached down to help her.

He pulled her up to him, his grip tight around her waist. He held her for a moment searching her face. His light blue eyes twinkled and a soft expression came over them.

Carolyn began to cry. She pointed toward Griff.

"Bunky's uncle. I mean nephew," she said.

"He tried to kill us," She continued as she started limping toward Griff. "And that bitch just took off!"

"No, no. The squad will be here soon. Who tried to kill you? Is he still here? What bitch?

"I dunno. I was in the well all night. But he's probably gone. He thinks I'm dead," she cried.

"Damn! Well let me check the house. You sit here. Right here! Don't you move!"

The caretaker hurried across the lawn and up the steps in a pace that belied his age, which looked to be about sixty.

"Things check out. Let's go. The cops should be here shortly."

"No! No cops. He'll kill me. He can't know I'm still alive!"

"Ok, Ok. Come on. Let's get you looked after. Where'd the bitch go?"

Carolyn responded with a long groan.

Just as they entered the front door, the whine of the approaching siren blared from the main road.

CAROL GOODNIGHT

Carolyn pulled away from the caretaker and opened the door to a large cabinet in the foyer. She crouched down and crawled in while the caretaker stood watching.

"Please! He will kill me!" she cried as she scoured his face for mercy.

"Ok. Ok," he said with a not-so-certain look as he headed out toward the approaching siren.

A short time later Carolyn heard men's voices coming into the house. They stopped on the porch just outside the open door.

"So you don't know what happened out here, Jas?" asked the deeper voice.

Carolyn peeked through the keyhole to see a large man in a sheriff's uniform tapping a cigarette on the shiny star on his chest. He tapped it seven or eight times before propping it in the corner of his mouth. He tilted his head and brought a small gun-shaped lighter from his pocket to light it before pulling in a slow, steady drag.

"Nope. Just drove in, like every other morning and found him like that. Just shot and laying out in the drive. I searched the house. No one else is here."

A third, younger voice said, 'I'll search the house, Captain."

"Nah, no need. Jas here said he already searched," the deeper voice responded.

"But Captain. This is official police business. He's not..." protested the younger voice.

"What he is, Snapper, is a Nam vet. Best brown-water minesweeper in the country. Go out with the ambulance."

"He's a dumbass," the sheriff said with a sigh. "Looks like the fella might pull through. Hopefully he can give us the shooter."

"Yeah," Jas replied as he noticed a drip of blood near the cabinet door. He walked to it, stepped on it, and then did a turn.

"Hey Jas. On the way out here I got a call from some I-talian guy name of Tomas from the Italian Secret Service. Says this guy has something to do with a case he's workin'. Keep him off my ass Jas, will ya? Don't need no international incident, if you know what I mean," the hefty policeman chuckled.

"Right," Jas replied with a shake of his head.

He closed the front door behind the Captain and went to the kitchen for a glass of water and a towel.

He opened the cabinet to find a wide eyed Carolyn staring back at him.

"Here," he said handing her the glass. "It's ok. How are you doing?"

"Tomas. He can't find me," she replied.

"Is he the guy that shot you?" asked the caretaker.

"No," she said, realizing that it would be difficult to explain her uneasiness at seeing Tomas. His father's death and now Paganelli's, and Ramone being shot were entirely her fault. She couldn't bear to face him. But before she could begin any explanation, the sound of footsteps on the front porch caused her to pull the cabinet door closed again.

Jas peered out the side-light to see a serious, dark haired man knocking with a sharp rap. From the small keyhole in the cabinet Carolyn watched Jas grip the door handle, lower his head, and take a deep breath.

She shook so hard that she had to set down the glass of water.

"Breathe," she whispered to herself.

"Aliberti," the man said as Jas opened the door.

Through the key-hole, Carolyn could see Tomas's wrinkled shirt and the day-old growth of beard on his tanned face. His rumpled appearance contrasted with his neat, slicked-back dark hair, tinged silver now at the temples. She watched as his expressionless, mahogany eyes, bearing the beginnings of crow's feet, took a sweep of the room.

Much lay beneath the surface of those tense, dark eyes. Deep, soulful eyes that hungrily embrace you while pulling you toward them. Reserved, tortured, glistening with sorrow, were a few thoughts that came to Carolyn's mind. His soul vibrated with taut, buried anger. Tomas had an aloof quality that Carolyn guessed was a reflection of the horrors in his past. He almost dared contact while at the same time pushed you away.

Carolyn had been correct in assuming that he had reasons for his rigid demeanor. Three shiny circular divots in his back—bullet holes—topped the list.

Tomas started to walk past Jas while introducing himself. Jas took a quick step to his left and pulled back his shoulders to block Tomas's path. Tomas stood back and glared at him.

"I'm AISE. I'm here to investigate several murders. You would be wise to cooperate with me," Tomas said.

"Near as I can tell, AISE or whatever, you're a fur piece from your jurisdiction," replied Jas as he lowered his chin and looked at Tomas dead in the eye. His full head of fluffy white hair dipped across his forehead in a James Dean swagger as his posture went from full-on military to don't fuck with me thug.

Tomas rolled his eyes.

"Ok, Ok. I get it. You're military. A bad ass. Look, I'm dealing with one crazy son-of-a-bitch here."

The siren blared again as the ambulance and police car rushed away. When Carolyn thought of Griff, a choke caught in her throat. He'd been shot in the back. And she'd heard another shot before Andrew had gotten to the well. The thought that Julep hadn't called for help lay in undisturbed anger deep inside her like a big, black coffin she was afraid to open.

Carolyn watched the two men walk toward the cabinet. Praying that the caretaker wouldn't expose her, she closed her eyes and wished it were all a dream.

"How'd you let this happen out here, Mr. Military? Sleeping on the job?" Tomas asked the caretaker.

Carolyn still hadn't breathed when she heard the caretaker reply, "That pride and ego down shit aint' gonna work on me, buddy. I vindicate myself to no man. Besides, I wasn't here. Just rolled up on it."

When Tomas said, "Um hum" a few times while Jas went on to vindicate himself nonetheless, Carolyn relaxed and took a breath.

"There's a woman tied up in all of this," Tomas finally interrupted. "Was anyone else here? This animal killed her brother and now she's in danger. He thinks her brother sent her information that could put him away forever."

"Nope, just the guy."

Tomas was quiet for a moment.

"He killed my father while looking for her," he said.

"Oh. You blamin' her?" Jas asked.

"No," Tomas said and then fell silent again.

"This killer has left a trail of bodies in his search for her. In addition to my father, he's killed my neighbor and shot another man from my town. Now this. Her fiancé."

"Oh, her fiancé? They say he might pull through." Jas said.

"This killer's next big deal is off the coast of Tunisia on Thursday with a powerful gunrunner. Ghet fah Mahryeed. I guess he thought he'd tie up his loose ends first. He made a stop at my father's vineyard to find Carolyn. That's when he killed my neighbor. I followed his trail here. He seems torn between vengeance and his illegal empire. At any rate, I'm going to kill him. For my father. For Paganelli. And for Carolyn."

"Carolyn. Is that her name?" Jas asked.

"Yes, Carolyn," Tomas repeated in a softened tone.

Then Carolyn heard his voice grow stern again.

"Listen, I have to search the house. With or without your cooperation. Your choice, but either way."

Jas led Tomas back through the entrance hall and up the stairs.

"Fine," he said. "I'll help you search. I actually didn't get to the attic yet, anyway. Let's start there. You need any help killin' that son-of-a-bitch, say the word, buddy. Just say the word."

CAROL GOODNIGHT

By the time they made it back down to the cabinet in the entry hall only blood drops and a glass of water remained.

Carolyn was gone. So was her rental car.

CHAPTER 8

Genoa, Italy

Landing in Genoa, clearing customs and immigration, Carolyn walked out the terminal building and hailed a Citroën cab idling nearby. She struggled to pull the cab door closed with her right arm by reaching across her body. The bullet, still embedded in her left arm, rendered it useless. It was numb aside from the deep throb. The one clean-through shot had been fortunate. Too bad she'd been shot twice.

But it could have been far worse, she thought with a shudder.

"Take me to the hospital in Santa Margherita Ligure, please," she said.

She had grabbed a jacket from Bunky's closet to cover her bloody blouse when she'd crept upstairs to retrieve her purse. She was thankful that Jas had somehow snookered Tomas into heading to the attic to begin his search.

She'd just had enough time to check her luggage and bandage her arm with shreds from her bloody blouse in the Charleston airport bathroom before her flight. She also checked on Griff before she took off. There was no information other than he was being admitted.

That was good news. She didn't want to spend too much time

pondering Griff's situation as she had more serious things to worry about now. That seemed cold, she knew, but she was cold. She didn't feel cold, she just was. Like frostbite. A frozen, dead burn.

She'd also made a call to Ramone to get his hospital information. She didn't want to stand around the lobby waiting for someone to direct her to the right place. She was afraid she'd faint. Then they'd find the bullet wounds and things would be fouled up. By law, bullet wounds must be reported to the police.

She knew from discussions with her brother that if bullets embed in soft tissue, for the most part, they could be left alone. The body will wall off the fairly inert metal without too much danger of inflammation or infection. Unless foreign bodies, such as cloth or wood harboring bacteria are introduced with the bullet, you're better off not digging around and possibly causing nerve damage. With a sudden sigh Carolyn realized how much she missed those grisly conversations with her brother.

She held her arm under the coat as she navigated the small hospital until she found the tiny white room. Ramone's face brightened when he saw her, but his smile quickly changed to a look of concern. She looked like hell; her long dark hair was stringy and her pretty blue eyes were gaunt and sunken. The oversized jacket with the large stain near the pocket that she'd noticed halfway across the ocean, didn't help.

Carolyn could see the alarm in his face and quickly smiled to assure him she was fine. The bullet pinched and pulled when she hugged him but she'd managed to turn her groan into a cryptic laugh.

"It was a long plane ride, Ramone. I know I look bad, but let's talk about you. What the hell happened? How are you?"

Carolyn sat back in the hospital chair and became quiet as Ramone recounted the day of the shooting. The evil thing in her soul was quiet as well; as it was paying rapt attention to Ramone's story and gobbling up every single word in gluttonous debauch.

The day started out as ordinary as any other day, he'd told her. But things took a quick turn by mid-morning. He was on the veranda enjoying a second cup coffee when a man walked up over the hill from the cemetery and startled him. Ombra, who had taken to laying on Augie's grave again since she'd left, had quit bellowing at sunrise and was walking next to the man.

Ramone explained that he recognized the young man as Antonio from San Fruttuoso. He knew about Ombra rescuing him. He admitted to Carolyn that he'd been bored and was happy to see him. He always had someone to chat with in town he said, as he was the go-to guy.

"It's very quiet up there, alone, Carolyn," he said with a look of concern.

Carolyn nodded.

He went on with his story. Antonio had come to visit and to thank Ombra again for saving his life.

"He was happy to hear about you and Mr. Griff getting married. Where is Mr. Griff?" Ramone asked.

"He's still in Charleston," Carolyn said matter-of-factly in an effort to avoid any further questions.

"Oh, "he responded, quite taken aback.

Carolyn nodded her head in an effort to have him move on, away from the subject of Griff.

Ramone explained he'd been in the kitchen pouring coffee for Antonio when he'd heard a buzz. The noise grew louder, to deafening, in a matter of moments. As he looked out the window, he saw Old man Paganelli's truck trailing a dirt storm, whizzing up the road toward the vineyard. Apparently he'd heard the noise too, and was headed up there in a hurry.

Ramone was alarmed, he explained. The entire town had been on watch after Augie's murder. He grabbed two rifles from Augie's gun rack and headed back to the veranda. He tossed one rifle to Antonio.

He took two full minutes to explain the horror on Antonio's face. All the young men know how to shoot, he'd told her. But practicing with your father behind the barn differs from being tossed a rifle in an unknown emergency. Apparently Antonio took the rifle and ran into the tall ryegrass that edged the trees behind the house.

"It was a big black helicopter! It landed in the front grass. I saw the guy jump out just as Paganelli got to the driveway. He took aim, Carolyn. And shot the truck! That far away! The truck veered off into the vines. Paganelli died instantly, they said."

Ramone grabbed a few tissues, buried his face, and sobbed. Carolyn took a tissue too. But a tough, angry grimace rather than tears filled her eyes.

Maybe she'd need the tissue, she thought. But probably for nothing more than to appear normal again.

She certainly didn't need a tissue for the cold, burning, vengeful creature she had now become.

"Paganelli was a good man," he said. "A great man!" He wept again.

When Ramone caught his breath, he looked down.

"I shot at the man. I missed," he choked. "He walked toward me, slow, and with a strange kind of limp. His eyes! I'll never forget those eyes! I just stood there!"

He grabbed more tissue.

From instinct, Carolyn reached over and squeezed his hand. She knew she should feel something along the lines of empathy and sorrow. She didn't. Her only awareness was of a growing steeliness.

"Antonio shot him. From the weeds. I ran. I was just to the trees when…" He lifted the sheet from his leg. His femur had been shattered.

Just then the door opened. They both looked up as Antonio walked in.

"I called him, Carolyn. He's staying at my place with Ombra. His parents are pissed but as long as he doesn't go back to the vineyard, they're ok with it. He can take you there. To my place."

"Ombra is gone," Antonio said apologetically as Carolyn shook his hand.

"I know where he is. Thank you, Ramone. You get well soon," Carolyn said. She stifled a groan as she bent to give Ramone a quick hug.

"Come on, Antonio. I'll give you a lift back to Ramone's. Do you still have that rifle?"

CHAPTER 9

Portofino, Italy

After hailing another cab and dropping Antonio at Ramone's apartment in town, she picked up her truck and some more heavy-duty antibiotics from the vet, supposedly for Ombra. She wasted little time in getting back to the vineyard. Her home. Yes, this was her home now, she realized.

She tried not to second guess herself for going to Charleston with Griff. She hadn't even hesitated when he'd made the plans.

She'd been in love, hadn't she? Or was she only looking for love to heal her heart again. What a mistake.

I'll call to check on him. Later, she thought and shook her head. She couldn't get the look on his face while grasping Julep's big childbearing hips out of her mind.

The old dirt road up to the vineyard was familiar, yet there was a weird strangeness about it now. Something seemed different. It was as if she were driving through an old photograph where the contrast had been darkened. The previous bright places were now filled with shadow. Nothing had changed in the landscape. She knew the change was within her.

After braking to a quick stop in front of the house, she sat paralyzed for a long while. The faded yellow stucco took on a luminous glow giving it a color rather like the spit of grasshopper tobacco. She stared across the withered vines trying not to think of Old man Paganelli, whose cottage she'd just passed. Ramone told her that Tomas had arranged for his burial behind the chapel near his father the day after tomorrow.

As the sun hissed into the sea, she felt in rhythm with its slow, steady descent.

Carolyn knew she should feel afraid of this change within her. But instead, she embraced the darkness with growing familiarity. It began to feel as comfortable as an old pair of socks.

As the trees slowly blurred into blackness, the howling began. As if in a trance, Carolyn stepped out of the truck and headed for the shed to get the gun Antonio had put there. She cradled the barrel over her right shoulder, gripped the rifle stock and winced from the pain in her arm while she looked for a flashlight. The thought of shooting a boar tonight quickened her pulse.

"Bastards," she said softly.

A calm flowed through her as she tramped the dark path to Augie's grave to find Ombra. The cool night air was rich with sweet, wet earthiness.

She'd never noticed the pungent undertone of murder until then. She almost dared a wild boar to attack her. Or anything else.

Ombra's haunting wail continued to pierce through the woods and echo out into the velvet evening filling it with sound. Her faint hollow footsteps on the stone floor as she passed through the chapel should have alerted the dog to her presence. But he continued in his lament.

By the moon's glow, she saw him lying on the soft hump of Augies final resting place. His head thrown back and his nose pointed north into the moon, he continued to bellow until she was almost to him. His howl became a yodeling whine before he snapped his giant maw shut and stared at her. The ears atop his great black, glossy body of bristling fur twitched as he slowly turned his head.

"What's this?" she asked firmly, unaffected by his doleful cries.

A gleam flashed through the night as he glanced toward her

with haunted, dejected eyes.

Carolyn sat at the foot of the grave next to the pitiful animal and sighed.

"I have to leave for a while, boy. I have to take care of something. I need you to behave. Do you hear me?" she asked firmly while gripping his head and looking into his big bewildered eyes.

The dog took a deep breath, let it out slowly, and put his head down.

"I'll try to come back to you. But if I don't, I don't want you up here wasting away. Do you understand?"

The dog lay with his head on his paws. He glanced over at her.

"Do you hear me?" she asked him louder.

He took in another deep breath and sighed again as he continued to stare into Carolyn's eyes.

"Okay then," she said.

She leaned over and rested on his back. Her arm ached. The dark thing was stoking the coals to keep the embers of her outrage aglow.

Without another sound, they both lay on Augies grave until dawn.

The chirping chorus of a small flock of black Merlis' hawking out a breakfast cry woke them from a fitful sleep. Carolyn buried her nose into Ombra's back. The scent of his thick fur brought the loss of Augie to her mind's eye with dagger sharpness. She drew the smell into her entire face

Before she stood to stretch the kinks from sleeping on the cold, hard ground next to her only friend, Carolyn reached over to the foot of the grave and pushed away a few handfuls of soil.

The leather pouch containing her silver rapier bracelet and the microchip lay waiting. She brushed it off as she stood up.

"Come on, boy!" she said firmly. Without a backward glance, she headed toward the house. Ombra caught up to her when she stepped off the path to pick a few wild flowers. The crisp biting radish scent of the purple crocus-like flower stung her nose as she tucked the stems behind her ear. She would later place them between the back pages of her passport to dry.

Her fingers, where she'd pulled the stems, began to tingle as she took a first sip of coffee. They were numb by the time she closed out her computer search of the islands off the coast of Tunisia.

After a quick shower and change of bandage, she replaced the microchip in the heart-shaped clasp and fastened the chain around her narrow ankle. When she'd first received it, she'd wondered why her brother sent an ankle chain. Why not a bracelet or necklace? But after finding the microchip it made more sense. It was far less obvious around her ankle. He must have planned to retrieve it himself. But just in case, he thought she'd figure it out. Open your heart. Look within.

Obvious now. What a fool I've been, she thought.

A memory of the wayward curls framing her brother's mischievous smiling face hit her so hard she slumped her shoulders. A thin slick of tear glistened her eyes, but only for a moment, before she grit her teeth and pursed her lips with resolve.

She packed the leather pouch with her passport and a few selected items of clothing in a large satchel and headed for the truck.

"Come on, Ombra."

Ombra sat back and lowered his head. His tail thumped slowly and he squinted in submission before averting his gaze.

"Come on!" Carolyn said firmly.

He sat frozen, darting his sad black eyes back and forth between Carolyn and the wall before wagging his tail again. This time at a quicker pace.

From somewhere within her peaked a slight shred of compassion. She knelt next to the dog and hugged his neck. A hint of moisture glistened her eyes again. She took another long sniff of his fur and then stood up.

CAROL GOODNIGHT

Antonio was sitting on the stoop in town when she drove up. She handed him a leash and a bag of food.

"Here's fifty dollars for dog food," she said reaching through her purse.

"Leash him near dusk. And thank you so much. I'm leaving the truck with you."

She bent and held the dog around the neck to smell him one last time.

"You behave!" she said and then stood up and headed for the harbor.

"Where are you going, Miss Carolyn?"

"Tunisia," she said over her shoulder.

Imaginary vulture wings thrummed a slow, steady tempo filling the empty space where Carolyn's soul had once resided. She tossed her satchel in the dinghy and unfastened the tie. The stubbing wings grew louder as she boarded The Kiss Goodnight, stowed the dink, and pulled up the anchor. With a flip of the switch and a swift turn, she motored out of the harbor.

She lifted her chin and faced into the wind. As she headed into the bright blueness, a thought about her new darkness came. As she contemplated it, she remembered a line from a children's story her mother often read to her and her brother at bedtime.

"You become."

Perhaps that's what happened when your velveteen got tattered and torn, she thought. *You become.*

The ever-present thrumming died down under the sound of the wooden yacht crashing through the water. But it was still present. And Carolyn knew it always would be. Until…

CHAPTER 10

If thou gaze long into an abyss, the abyss will also gaze into thee.

Friedrich Nietzsche

A pair of peregrine falcons fighting and clawing a small catch spiraled above the craggy sun baked cliffs. Carolyn watched as they soared upward toward the sweet chestnut trees on the forested ridge of the northern slope.

A small group of hikers on the outer shore, all wearing matching yellow sweatshirts, waved from the Mediterranean scrub while resting along the trail of former mule tracks. A damp morning wind blew in from the west. Carolyn's sail billowed a snapped reply as she glided past the rocky promontory out of Portofino bay.

Her anger, bred years ago in the frightening midnight hours while hiding behind the couch of her dysfunctional childhood home, sizzled through her veins. As a young girl she'd mastered the technique of keeping these embers under careful control in fear of a bursting flame surge that might consume her.

The gathered fragments of firewood tossed through the portal of her very own personal hell had smoldered her entire life, until now. Now it was unleashed with a deadly purpose that served nicely to sharpen her focus and intensity.

CAROL GOODNIGHT

If the winds kept up to at least ten knots she figured it'd take about two days to cross the three hundred nautical miles to the Galite islands off the coast of Tunisia. As it was, she was moving along at almost twelve.

The dark sunglasses and her hat tipped low helped to shade Carolyn's eyes. She stood braced at the helm not making a move for well over two hours. The Kiss Goodnight glided under cloud-threaded Versace blue skies. Salt air whipped Carolyn's long, dark ponytail against her sun-burnished skin.

"You're starting to look like an overripe blackberry," her mother used to say. But Carolyn quickly quieted the gentle voice in her head and threw another memory of Andrew on the fire.

The book, she remembered. He'd given her a rare copy of Paradise Lost.

"To read to our children," he'd said.

But her room had been ransacked, and the book stolen the very next day.

"No need to call the police," she remembered him saying. He'd take care of it. She was certain now that he had, indeed, taken care of it.

Shades of black looming on the horizon jutted from the sea. Following around the Northern Cape of Corsica, Carolyn sailed toward St. Florent.

Hemmed in by towering dark mountains, the quaint Corsican seaside town snuggled along the honey-gold crescent beach that provided natural protection from the open sea. She could have stopped at Calvi and saved a bit of time, but she'd been there with Griff on their romantic adventure and she didn't need to provoke yet another ember to her flaming anger. She needed to keep her fire in check for the days ahead.

Maybe I should have called to check on Griff before I left.

Or maybe not, she thought and shrugged.

Carolyn motored in, bore left to the marina and docked near the larger ships. After a quick tie-up and trip to customs she headed down the ramp toward the cheerful bayside shops.

A shadow of wings passed high overhead, turned and then dipped low to swoop by her. As the bird passed, his cold, corvid eyes glared into her face. His furtive stare was full of warning. She was sure of it. It had caught her step. The bird alighted on the mooring cleat of the last slip and waited. As Carolyn approached, he raised his nape feathers, hunched his back and flexed his wing and tail feathers in a warning display. As she got closer, he lunged his head toward her and the dark circle of his pupils increased and decreased in size so quickly it reminded her of a whirligig.

"Hm," she murmured as she kept an eye on him while passing.

She wasn't sure if there had actually been a crow at that well in Charleston that caused her to take a life's breath, or if it had only been in her mind. But she was sure that this raven, with his straight, sharp beak and midnight plumage was a symbol of death. However, she didn't care. She was confident enough in her anger that she could overcome any challenge in her quest for revenge.

She ignored the bird's admonition and stepped from the dock.

Only a hint faded, a few leather-brown tourists sat at shabby-chic wooden tables strung along the waterfront. It wasn't crowded this time of year and Carolyn was pleased. Apparently she was becoming one of the snobby locals, she thought with amusement.

Wonderful aromas of barbecue mixed with saline air tantalized her taste buds as she headed to check in with the harbor master. Before ordering lunch though, she stopped in a small stylish hat shop next to the Pharmacia.

Loud cat-call whistles from the ally beside the store caused the owner to come out and chastise the young workers loading a truck.

"Boys! Scram you buggers! Sorry, madam. These boys!" said the shopkeeper. "How may I help you?"

"Do you have anything in the Tunisian style?" Carolyn answered.

"We have everything!" said the shopkeeper.

Two hours later, the shopkeeper slipped a shopping bag into Carolyn's newly henna-tattooed hand and wished her well.

"Your love will be more than pleased, my dear," she said. "Remember the trick to slip the scarf. Very nice for the honeymoon."

Carolyn smiled.

After ordering, Carolyn sat in the shade under the bright lime-green parasol at a nearby quayside restaurant and waited for lunch. She admired how the dappled shadows between the slatted wooden chairs played on the patterns of her new artwork. The crushed leaves and stems of the henna plant used as a stain would last a few short weeks. A small part of her wondered if she'd live that long.

Get that thought out of your mind! she thought. *I will live. But someone else may not...*

For years Carolyn had been fascinated by the exotic mehndi art and Arabic patterns adorning the glamourous women in this region of the world. Her brother's stories had provoked an interest in their cultural traditions.

The intricate design wound from her fingers to half way up her left arm. The shopkeeper was surprised and then amused when Carolyn also had her stain the black wings and skull of a raven in the hollow of her lower back. She sat stiff straight so her blousy shirt wouldn't remove the paste until the stain was set.

"Death," she whispered.

"Pardon, madam?" asked the waiter returning with her lunch.

"My tattoo." she said smiling and holding her arm higher.

Her other arm, held limply at her side and covered under a long sleeve, bore the extensive and not-quite-so-artsy purple-yellow smear of an ugly bruise accentuated by the dusky edges of three gaudy bullet holes.

She pulled a large prescription bottle from her purse. The

patient name read: Canine Ombra. She swallowed another two giant capsules.

CAROL GOODNIGHT

CHAPTER 11

With her bag slung over her shoulder, Carolyn stepped away from the rack of postcards and lifted her face into the afternoon sun. She waited for the oncoming jeep to pass before stepping across the narrow street to the dock.

In addition to her new purchases, her bag held half of a crisp-tender duck sandwich on a thick bun of black squid-ink bread and a bundle of julienned strips of white scallion, daikon radish and fresh cucumber tucked in paper thin tortilla-like pancakes. Leftovers for dinner later.

The approaching jeep jerked to a stop next to Carolyn and a chubby young man hopped out. Initially, she thought it was the boys from the loading truck stopping to make a few more cat calls.

The driver, a tall thin man with a severely sharp nose, shouted, "See I told you it was her!"

The chubby man stepped behind her with a bumbling lurch. He took a tight grip on her wounded arm and shoved a knife against her back. Carolyn went pale as the pain seared through her body. Her lips pulled back in a grimace causing her to bare her teeth as she sucked in a gasp. She stumbled as the man pushed her toward the jeep.

Never be taken to crime scene number two, she remembered from a long ago self-defense class or a late night crime drama.

"Help!" she screamed

The driver shook his head and reached under his seat. He stretched his arm toward her revealing a shiny purple Taser. An electric pulse zapped her in the stomach.

"Dumb ass, I told you to use the Taser!" the hawk-nosed man said to his partner.

Carolyn stiffened as her entire body tensed rigid in one big cramp. Her arms jerked into her ribs as they drew in close to her body. The muscles in her neck tightened and burned as they hunched her shoulders up toward her ears. She visualized King Kong beating her spine with a four by four at the same time lightning bolted through her. She couldn't move.

When the zap ceased, she bent over and slumped toward the ground. The chubby man pushed her into the back of the jeep where she plopped on the seat. He picked her feet up and shoved them inside before hopping in next to her.

After a brief unconsciousness, she became aware of everything happening. Still unable to move, her face bounced on the back jeep seat while they zipped through the waterfront market area and then made a quick left. It happened so fast that the other patrons still had their mouths open.

Through the grog, she watched them turn near a flashing green sign above a pizza joint before heading up out of the business district. The drool on her face tickled her chin as they flew over bumps in the dirt road. She closed her mouth and continued to lay silent as her sensations slowly came back. The intense odor of fresh onions and cilantro filled the back seat of the jeep. The fat man holding her down must have just finished a diet salad for lunch. Had he eaten it with his hands, she absently wondered?

It wasn't long before they came to a stop and a garage door opened.

"Are you sure the guy still has a reward out for her? I mean, that was last summer, man."

"Shut up, Asshole. I know what I'm doing. I can't believe she sailed in here like that, with that stupid yacht. The Kiss Goodnight. Every swingin' dick lookin' to make a dime is on the lookout for that boat."

"Well, we need to contact the guy and get her out of here before your mom gets home. I wonder why she didn't change the name."

"I told you to shut up!"

Before the garage door lowered, Carolyn glanced around. Parked just inside the door was a scooter. She thought she saw the keys. She continued to lay still and bide her time.

"Here, hold the Taser on her while I go look for the contact info. I'm sure I have it written down on her picture in my room."

"Well, hurry up," said the guy in the back seat as he stuffed the purple cylinder in his front pocket.

When his partner shook his head with a heavy sigh, he shrugged his shoulders and said, "Whaaaat? She's still passed out!"

As soon as the driver entered the house and the door to the garage closed shut behind him, Carolyn jumped up, dove into the front seat, and hit the garage door remote. The guy in the back seat shook his head. He was so surprised that he sat paralyzed for a second. As he pulled the Taser from his pants, he hit the zap button and began tasing himself.

Carolyn lunged out of the jeep and just before falling on her face, her rubbery legs came to life. She scrambled along the floor using her one good arm on the concrete to keep balance as she headed for the scooter. The door was almost up when she hopped on.

"Yes!" she cried, although it came out sounding more like a wet garbled "yeths."

As she turned the key, the door to the house opened and the tall, thin driver screamed.

"You fucking asshole!"

The other guy, bent over in the back seat was still convulsing. Despite the biting pain in her arm, Carolyn hung on tight as the bike swerved back and forth down the driveway. She quickly glanced back to see the driver pounding the other man in the face. She tried hard to hold the small scooter steady with her spongy legs as she zipped through the streets looking for the main thoroughfare to the business district.

"Yes!" she cried again, a little clearer this time, when she saw the flashing green sign of the pizzeria. She slid her foot out, kicking up rocks as she skidded around the turn, and then gunned it for the straight-a-way. Instead of driving on the street, she turned onto the pedestrian path that took her directly to the dock.

She glanced back to see people darting out of the way of the boys following in the jeep. They had to stop when they made it to the ramp, as the vehicle wouldn't fit through the walkway. When she looked back again, she saw the two men running after her on foot.

She skidded up to The Kiss Goodnight, slowed a bit, and stuck her foot out. At the same moment she stepped off, she gripped the throttle to give the bike more juice. The back wheel scratched against her calf before it left the dock. It arched through the air. She was still gaining her balance when it landed in the water. An oblong outline of bubbles glub, glubbed to the surface as she threw off the dock lines.

The engine of The Kiss Goodnight roared to life as she watched the two men running down the dock toward her. With a barely perceptible ripple, the beautiful yacht glided away just as the two would-be kidnappers reached her slip. She throttled up full blast and took off.

The hell with the wake, she thought.

Looking back through the furrow of the two diverging wave surges, she saw a dock-hand point to a spot in the water still bubbling. The tall thin man punched the chubby one again. After clearing the last marina signal, she looked down and noticed the shopping bag with her leftover lunch still dangling around her shoulder. Beneath her grimace, a grin began to curl at the corners of

CAROL GOODNIGHT

mouth.

KISS OF THE NAKED LADY

CHAPTER 12

The brisk breezes of the mistral winds, characteristic of winter afternoons on the west coast of Corsica, made for uncomfortable swells as Carolyn continued motoring down the coast.

These winds were responsible for the exceptional sunny conditions and the desert-like vegetation in this charming and relatively undiscovered part of the French Riviera. The mistral usually sweeps the coast with pleasant breezes evoking colorful romantic images. The dry cold air clears the sky to an unbelievable shade of blue.

But when the mistral blows steady, the howling sets most people on edge, causing restless sleep and uneasiness in the soul.

Uneasiness was the best of what was in Carolyn's soul now.

Every swingin' dick lookin' to make a dime is on the lookout for that boat. Those words came back to her as she set the yacht to auto pilot. Her arm was bleeding again and she thought briefly about trying to dig out the bullet. She found Griff's old Mickey Mouse T-shirt in the master bedroom and tore it in five-inch-wide shreds. This size would cover all three holes. And she had to admit, it felt great to tear his shirt to shreds. When she finished ripping, she poured herself a glass of vodka and sat on the lounge.

The constant smooth blowing of the Mistral wind felt good on her warm skin and she enjoyed it despite the howling. She wondered if she had a fever. She took a gulp of Vodka and held up her arm to admire the Mehndi tattoo. With a graceful swirl, she practiced the exotic flowing hand movements she'd learned from the shopkeeper. Not able to move her right arm without pain, she settled for a slow swivel of her shoulder.

Before downing another shot of Vodka, she picked up the Mickey Mouse shreds. She doused one strip in Vodka to wipe away the dribbling blood. With one end of fabric between her teeth, she began to wrap. Two of the holes looked like miniature pizzas ringed in a dried out crust. They looked fine. Well, as fine as two pizza-like bullet holes can look. The exit hole on the inner side of her elbow dripped fresh blood from its gray-black rim.

When she finished bandaging her reinjured arm, she noticed one large Mickey Mouse eye staring at her with a look of surprise.

Surprised at what? That she didn't know Andrew was still alive.

She took another swig.

"Damn Griff," she muttered as if he were responsible for Mickey's accusing one-eyed glare.

The wounds felt better wrapped but the dull ache continued.

Swingin' dicks, she thought again. She knew she'd have to think about what she'd heard.

"Why didn't she change the name? Everyone is looking for The Kiss Goodnight."

She rustled around the storage room, the third berth Augie had changed into a large closet, until she found an old can of black paint. She remembered the day Ramone changed the name of the yacht. Bittersweet, now.

"Forget it," she said and threw aside an old tackle box.

The second can was underneath the jerry-rigged scaffolding ropes. A half-cleaned crusty-stiff paint brush stuck to the side of the can. She hauled it all on deck, turned off the engine, and set the anchor.

None of the name changing lore would help her now.

Perhaps Neptune would forgive her under the circumstances.

She lowered the deck stairs.

"Nothing worse than being in the middle of the ocean next to your boat with the steps up," she remembered Augie warning.

A diffuse band of clouds belted the horizon as the sun set in a flaming orange disc, like a piece of avulsed flesh resembling a perfectly round lacerated gash of hell. She took another swig of vodka and lowered the scaffold.

***

A dim red light from the cabin cast a glow on the wind-whipped rush of water passing against the hull. The gentle sound was a slight distraction while Carolyn counted the hours until the sun would show her face again. She lie awake in the early morning darkness trying to quiet the alarm sounding in her mind. The dark hollows beneath her eyes grew deeper as her thoughts spun in an endless vortex.

Stars stretching across the universe flickered through blackness as the moon smoldered in its eternal march across the heavens. All the while that old Witchy Pitchfork endlessly stirred the brew in her big black pot. She remembered when she and her brother had given that name to the figure in the moon. Witchy Pitchfork. Even with her eyes squeezed tight she could see that witch. That old witch.

Stirring.

Forever stirring.

The frown on Carolyn's face grew deeper as she hunched her shoulders and pulled into a ball. She folded her arms around herself as her wounded limb throbbed. She stared out into the night, brooding and absorbed in thought.

Between the shadows of the howling flap of sails she sensed the image of Andrew's lifeless eyes. The utter emptiness in them could swallow a person whole.

She tried to focus on the clew of the boom to decipher a pattern. Anything to bring rest, relief, blessed unconsciousness. Even for a moment.

Low clouds gathered to dim the moonlight and after a while her heavy lids fluttered.

In an empty ocean, she tried to allow herself twenty minutes of sleep at a time. She reasoned that it would take that long for a fast ship to crest over the horizon and run her down. But who was she kidding? Twenty minutes of sleep would have been a blessing.

Her eyes finally draped closed and floated her away on a tide of deep blue. And for a time, a short time, there were no thoughts, no pain, no tears. It was as if she didn't exist.

Before dawn, the monotonous clanging of the halyard tapping against the mast provoked her fully awake. With the horizon still empty, she started a pot of coffee and then weighed anchor on the newly christened Eleganza. Hopefully the stale half-bottle of the leftover bubbly she and Griff shared on their engagement day would appease the god of the deep.

The winds blew at fourteen knots and with any luck she'd be near the La Galite islands of Tunisia before dark.

Near the gunrunner Ghet fah Mahryeed and his planned meeting with Andrew.

Nearer to her revenge.

She arranged the sails at an angle to the keel and then braced the yards forward by slackening the starboard and pulling on the port braces. Then she pulled the lowest sheets aft. With the bow facing directly west and her sails trimmed, she hauled the wind four points and navigated a path to avoid Asinara, the steep, rocky, sinus shaped island off the Northwestern tip of Sardinia.

At one time the island was a notorious maximum-security prison as well as a quarantine station for Cholera victims. Today it was a national park and breeding ground for turtles and silky-haired wild sheep. Its most famous resident and namesake, the albino donkey, can be seen climbing cliff-side crags if you dare to veer close enough.

Once she passed the island, she was able to steer a more direct course toward Tunisia. For another hour or so she clipped along making small course changes as needed to keep on the Southwest tack. With the breeze always behind her, it was hugely satisfying to cover so much distance.

At noon she sailed between the flat, dusty seaside town of Portoscuso on Sardinia and the small fishing village of Carloforte on the lush island of San Pietro. She gazed at the island and thought of Griff.

Nestled between palm trees on the busy waterfront and the lush, forested hillside, the butter-yellow buildings curved in a crescent around the harbor.

She and Griff would've stopped there, she thought.

Bright fishing boats bobbed in the marina while shafts of sunshine and shadow dappled between the narrow passageways zigzagging up the cobbled streets to nowhere. Carolyn sighed. The open windows with neighbors visiting, and couples walking along the shops reminded her that she'd given up any feelings of love and longing. Even the thought of Griff didn't cause her heart to lurch any longer. Her hopes and plans for a future meant nothing now. Her life stretched out in a hollow black void.

A scattering of white cumulonimbus clouds overhead drifted in front of the sun from time to time blocking the rays of the sun. Carolyn looked up.

This would be an excellent day for revenge.

The yacht steadily cruised through the frothy brine as the salt air whipped and whistled through the spars and rigging. Carolyn's hair lashed at her face. The sails whined a melancholy tune as they billowed her across the glimmering expanse toward the far reaches of the Mediterranean.

For a second, as if from a dream, Carolyn thought she heard a whining sound. An ominous voice. Warning her, pleading with her, to turn back.

Words on the wind, she thought as she cruised forward into the unknown.

"I was wrong," she said to herself.

"This dark emptiness isn't my only companion. I now have revenge to keep me company."

Carolyn sensed Andrew's presence ahead, not much further now. Appealing and fascinating on the surface, he was turbulent and unforgiving at his depth. She would have thought him like the sea in that regard, but that would've been too great a compliment for what Andrew was.

So, with the keystone-cop kidnappers behind her and her one true enemy ahead, she held a steady compass course and watched as the pencil marks on her chart edged south, toward the sparse and dangerous North African coast. Chained like a monkey to an organ grinder she danced to the tune of her vengeance. Andrew's name had been penned next to this siren song on her dance card somewhere in eternity.

A hot dry wind blew North across the barren group of rocks jutting from the sea a little over 20 miles off the coast of Tunisia. It was late afternoon when The Kiss Goodnight glided within sight of her destination. It wasn't hard to distinguish her target among the six island archipelago, as there was a lookout tower on the top of one island's cone shaped peak, just as described on her internet search. Ruins from a church and a few Genoese building remnants scattered the hill alongside a dirt road that led away from the flat landfall used for docking.

Carolyn eased the mainsail until the yacht stopped all forward motion. She put the rudder over hard to windward and fastened it well, taking care that the boat did not go head to wind. She watched through several cycles of wave-swell patterns before deciding to drop the mainsail as the yacht had tended to climb windward. She breathed deeply while keeping a close eye on it. Her hands shook as she reached in the bin for her binoculars. In an attempt to steady her nerves, she held tight to the doorframe.

"Stop shaking!" she admonished herself.

Fiddling with the binocular focus helped. A calmness washed over her as she looked up through the lenses.

The steep, rugged island was accessible only from its southwest side by a small skiff, or by air from a helicopter. The internet claimed that the island had been sold to a sugar conglomerate for fourteen million dollars. Satisfied with the yacht's position, she steadied the binoculars. She wondered if that price had included Hade's Lair, the name Ghet fah Mahryeed had given to his concrete, steel, and glass hide-a-way manse.

Clutching the rocky hillside, it sat haunched like the ribcage of a giant prehistoric monster threatening to strike. Enormous cantilevered concrete columns fanned out, overlapping one another to form a roof line. The exterior walls consisted of giant two-story plates of glass that curved seamlessly into each other.

The place could've been used in a James Bond movie. A creepy hairless cat would fit in quite well.

At the pinnacle of the island stood a round, fortified drum tower that could have existed in antiquity. Carolyn watched gun barrels aim toward her from the turret as a white-uniformed soldier scurried down the hillside toward the house. He reminded her of a phantom mountain goat. Carolyn trained the binoculars toward the gun barrels. Only a yellow lens and a flash of light from scope reflections was visible on the sniper drawing down on her.

She dropped her vision toward the house. The phantom goat man stood on the terrace pointing at her. The man he was speaking to, with his waving hands and authoritative posture as he glared out toward her yacht, suggested he was the man in charge. Ghet fah Mahryeed. The corners of Carolyn's lips rose in a nervous smile, just enough to give her an amused look. She headed down to get ready.

The engine of the inflatable skiff grew louder as she tucked a small dried flower in her hair. She wrapped a silk scarf around her head, twisting and tying it the way the woman from St. Florent had shown her. She found herself humming.

The luxurious fabric in an ocean palette highlighted with shades of fiery sunset and gleaming silver was a glamorous disguise for her crushed poison flower. Next, she tied a matching scarf across the bullet holes on her arm. She then twirled around the room letting the sumptuous fabric flow before catching it and tying it to cover her naked body.

After one last slow turn to check her reflection, she was satisfied.

She dabbed a little color on her nose and freshened her deep coral lipstick before she heard the footsteps onboard.

Carolyn smiled at the young military-looking man as she stepped from the cabin. She slowly turned her face upward toward the cantilevered terrace. One of the richest men in the world was glaring down at her. Weak in the knees, she whispered under her breath, "The time has come."

She kept her gaze upward and slowly spun her back toward Ghet fah Mahryeed. As the rays of sun set stage over the horizon with a radiant glow, it shimmered upon Carolyn's bronzed skin as she held her exotically stained hand in the air with a hypnotizing swirl.

With a fanciful twist, she brushed her other hand in a swaying motion next to her hip. She unhitched the small knot at her waist. The scarf blew out across the sea, anchored only by the tight wrapping around her bullet ridden arm. The guard immediately dropped his eyes, but not before his gaze lingered on the raven skull and flared wings artfully painted on the delicate curve of her lower back.

"This is private domain, mam. No one intrudes without an

invitation."

"I think if you check, you'll find me on the guest list," she said with feigned confidence.

The guard fumbled with his walkie-talkie. After a few garbled exchanges, he nodded toward the skiff.

Carolyn rewrapped the scarf around her body and grabbed her satchel. As she followed the man to the skiff, she slipped loose the rudder on her yacht and took a deep breath.

CAROL GOODNIGHT

CHAPTER 13

A strange game, the only winning move is not to play

-Wargames

Two large German shepherds barking and straining at the leash met the small inflatable as it arrived at the flat spit of land serving as a dock. The dogs snarled and growled, hunkering low to ground, pulling back their lips to show their teeth. The guard holding them became more tangled as the dogs lurched forward. Just before all three fell into the ocean, the man on the inflatable gave a command. The dogs sat stone-still.

Carolyn's bare feet burned on the hot rocks as she stepped ashore. But she held her smile firm as she looked up toward the veranda. The man with the binoculars frowned at her. Carolyn winced when the guard from the inflatable grabbed her arm. She jerked away from him, stood tall, and held up her chin. Her eyes squinted and she stared at him before turning her glare to the terrace.

The man on the terrace lowered his binoculars. His two wide eyes and round mouth, almost covered by his thick mustache, took on a curious expression before he doubled over in a belly laugh.

"Welcome to Hade's Lair," he bellowed.

"Please escort that beautiful creature up here. And be gentle!"

he commanded the guard.

Carolyn bent to slide on the sandals from her bag. She'd made the dramatic entrance and purloined the invitation she'd hoped to receive. No sense burning her feet. Before heading up the steep climb she double knotted the scarf.

"Welcome! Welcome to my humble abode," said the gentleman. The color of his face, the part that wasn't covered by his thick, groomed mustache was a dark tan. His skin was the color of the people from this region, but looked enhanced, possibly by many hours on a golf course. As for his dress, it was impeccable. His shirt, long sleeve despite the heat, was starched white and rolled back twice at the cuff. Just enough to show the flash of dazzling black onyx cufflinks.

"I am Ghet fah Mahryeed. And what manner of devilish creature are you that approaches my shore?" he asked.

But for the few wisps of silver around his temples, his hair gleamed jet black. The flickering light caught the slight movement as he spoke, causing his hair to reflect like the slow-motion flapping of glistening bat wings. She guessed him to be around fifty, maybe a little older, it was hard to tell.

Carolyn lowered her chin and looked up toward the handsome man. His deep black eyes locked with hers. She stretched out her tattooed arm and presented her dainty hand. His response was to bring her fingers to his lips. His gaze never left her face.

"I am Eleganza," she replied.

"Ah, the same as your boat. And just as lovely," he said as he opened an ornate cigarette case and extended the neat flat cigarettes toward her.

"Egyptian, blended especially for me."

Carolyn shook her head.

"And what brings you to my waters?" he asked.

He slipped a flat brown cigarette between his lips, licking the tip before dangling it at the corner of his mouth.

"Oh, your waters?" she said and laughed.

Carolyn watched him slide the slender gold case into his pocket and retrieve an ornate ruby-and-gold lighter before she continued.

"I'm on a voyage. You see, I recently lost my finance," she said, adding a somber note to her voice.

"We were to be married this week. He was killed in a senseless auto accident in the U.S. I'm sailing to assuage my grief."

She was on a voyage to assuage something. But it wasn't grief this time.

Mahryeed took a drag on his cigarette before flicking it over the terrace. He then lifted her hands to his face and kissed her fingers again, this time grasping them together.

"My dear, you have suffered much. I am sorry for your loss. Please join me for dinner. I have a guest arriving from America shortly. My business with him will be concluded after dinner and I will be more than delighted to distract you from your sorrow."

"From America?" Carolyn asked.

"Ah yes. He's a delightful bore. So full of himself. So arrogant. But that's the price of business, I fear. You can't pick your customers."

"What is it you sell, if I may ask?"

"Mostly sugar. But we can talk about all that later. Crandall!" he called just as a tall, solid woman entered the room.

"Crandall, show Miss Eleganza to the guest quarters where she may freshen up. I'll see you at eight o'clock," he said as he kissed her fingertips again. The glint from his black onyx cufflinks mesmerized her for a moment before she looked up to his face and found his eye contact more of the leer she'd been expecting all along.

Carolyn followed the servant through a front entry that could have easily welcomed an elephant or two.

Huge concrete structural pillars and endless curves of glass blended to resemble a giant otherworldly spaceship. The entrance towered three stories high. Polished concrete floors gleamed under the opulent handmade Persian carpets staged around the large foyer and into the entrance hall.

Floor to ceiling sheers billowed in the main room flickering light from the sunset against the shadow from the surrounding rock. The furnishings were a combination of handcrafted heavy wood-and-stone to delicate ultra-modern. Other than the light tapping of Carolyn's sandals and the squish-scrunch of Crandall's sensible rubber-soled shoes, there was no sound in the house. No air-conditioner noise, no refrigerator humming, nothing. The silence only thickened as Carolyn followed the lumbering servant further into the house.

Crandall led her through the dining area toward the kitchen. She was a large woman and although she looked to be almost sixty, Carolyn imagined her to be every bit as tough as the guards. Especially the one with the dogs. Her rheumy, bloodshot eyes, like two dead oysters generously topped with tabasco ice, peered from her sallow moon-shaped face in a constant expression of sullen distaste.

She was probably the head of the household staff and Carolyn wondered how that arrangement might have come about. Her wiry gray hair, brushed backward from her face, highlighted wet, gray eyes didn't blink. At all.

"Will you be having red wine, like the other American?" she asked with a condescending accent on the word American.

"May I see the wine?" Carolyn responded as they headed through the kitchen.

Crandall sighed. "Of course you may. You are a guest," she said as she led her to the butler's pantry. I'll have someone bring a few choices from the wine cellar. Mr. Mahryeed only drinks champagne," she said in a proprietary tone.

"Please make your choice quickly. Dinner will be served in one-half hour. And Mr. Mahryeed is prompt."

CAROL GOODNIGHT

Carolyn wasn't sure it was possible, but Crandall's look of disapproval grew deeper.

"Will anyone else be joining us?"

"No," Crandall replied, not bothering to hide her snarl as she left to see about the wine.

A decanter of red wine, presumably for Andrew, sat airing on the counter. Carolyn reached in her scarf and pulled out the small dried flower. She crushed it into the glass and watched the white powder float through the dark red liquid as it dissolved. The last trace had disappeared before Crandall arrived with several bottles clutched in her muscular arms.

Carolyn chose a light rose' and set it in front of the red wine decanter. Crandall set the other bottles down with grunt. Carolyn was almost certain she'd heard a growl as Crandall's murky dead eyes motioned toward the back of the kitchen.

She followed the large woman up an elegant stairway and after several more sighs and grunts; she stopped in front of a double door leading to a large circular bedroom. She huffed again, still with no perceivable blink, and reminded Carolyn that dinner would be in one half hour before she left.

The smooth, curving concrete and granite mushroom-shaped structure in the center of the room served as a wall support that doubled as a fireplace. A small light illuminated an eerie shadow on the back wall where a story-and-a-half of bookshelves had seven or eight books centered toward the top. A step further into the room and she discovered the origin of the shadow. The only organic matter in the room, it was a sinister looking black orchid that resembled a black bat in flight. Carolyn stood before the floor-to-ceiling windows circling half of the room. Only the satin sheen from the last glow of sunset and the silhouette of constantly blowing scrub grass on the windswept hillside was visible in the vast emptiness stretching out over the dark ocean. No sign of The Kiss Goodnight.

She was on her own now. This was it. If everything went well, and Andrew swallowed the poisoned wine, there would surely be repercussions. Of course Mahryeed would suspect her. She didn't care. It'd be worth it.

Just then the blinding lights and noise from a helicopter surrounded the island as it flew by her window.

"He's here," she muttered under her breath.

Carolyn took a deep breath and opened her bag. The long, blue velvet gown slid over her body in a soft, cool flow. She'd looked long and hard to find a gown similar to the one she'd worn that New Year's Eve when Andrew choked her. She hoped seeing her again, alive, and in this gown would make him choke.

And if that didn't do it, perhaps the poison currently airing in his decanter would do the trick. The delicate snake rapier bracelet added a much needed flair to the outfit. She regretted not having it the first time around.

She pulled her hair in an upsweep and applied a touch more eyeliner. After checking herself in the mirror, she smiled. Even the dusky bullet holes showing in the sleeveless gown couldn't detract from how similar she looked on that fateful night.

The beginning of the end. But it hadn't been the beginning, really. The beginning was when he'd killed her brother.

"Well, this will be the end. One way or the other," she said to herself.

Angle-like voices drifted up from the first floor as she entered the hall. Lacrimosa, the Requiem Mass in D Minor by Mozart grew louder as she descended the stairway. She'd heard the music once before, while passing an open church in New Orleans shortly after her brother passed away. Mesmerized by the sinister tones she'd stepped into the church to find herself in the midst of a funeral. She'd made a quick exit. Along with most of her other experiences in New Orleans, the music disturbed her. Her slow steps glided down the staircase in tune with the haunting rhythm as she approached her biggest fear: Death.

CAROL GOODNIGHT

Carolyn halted just outside the dining room. The raucous guffaw of Andrew's sharp, staccato laugh overpowered the orchestra's dramatic crescendo.

He's putting on his show, probably considering himself exceptionally amusing. As usual.

"Well, my friends," she heard Mahryeed interrupt. "Let's toast to another lucrative deal. And then I want to introduce you to a lovely new guest."

"A lovely guest?" she heard Andrew ask as the glasses clinked. Carolyn could feel her pulse throbbing through her neck. She stepped around the corner as Andrew swallowed a large, unmannerly gulp of wine.

"Ah, Eleganza! Meet my guests," Mahryeed said with his glass still held high.

CHAPTER 14

"Revenge, the sweetest morsel to the mouth that ever was cooked in hell."

Walter Scott, The Heart of Mid-Lothian

Carolyn stepped into the room to receive the shock of her life. She stopped, motionless as if her brain had short-circuited. She didn't understand. The color drained from her face and her eyebrows raised to form a deep crease in her forehead. A harsh, hollow gasp escaped her trembling lips.

At the table with Mahryeed and Andrew sat Tomas. He'd just sipped from his glass of red wine.

Carolyn quickly scanned the room to see only one red wine decanter. The look of horror on Tomas's face when he saw her matched her own. Apparently she wasn't the only one here for revenge.

"Tomas!" she screamed.

Everything moved fast-forward from there. A loud crash came from the butler's pantry.

Andrew jerked stiff in his chair. His face glazed crimson a

split-second before his unblinking eyes bulged from the sockets with a death stare. His lips pursed together and moisture drooled in the deep crevices forming his frown.

The look of him made her cringe with fear. She stumbled against the doorway.

Andrew's eyes squinted as his loud shriek rang through the house.

"Bitch!" he screamed.

Tremors overtook his sweating grimace and both of his arms shook as he flung himself forward in a deep, choking cough.

Mahryeed's face twitched. His mouth, slightly open, quivered as if he were trying to form a word. His eyes locked Carolyn in a gaze of piercing destruction, ready to kill. He gaped from one to the other of his guests, trying to figure out what was happening. It only took seconds before he realized he'd been set-up in some way. He pushed back on his chair.

Tomas jumped toward him, grabbed him by the back of his neck and slammed his skull on the thick glass table. Mahryeed, stunned for a second, reached around sideways and punched Tomas in the gut. Tomas raised his elbow and smashed it into the high soft spot of Mahryeed's temple. He held the back of his neck waiting to see if he would move again. He didn't.

Andrew, mid cough, suddenly slumped and then went rigid. His chin dropped to his chest. His eyes stared out sideways glaring at the wall before they disappeared under his lids. He dropped to the floor like a tree trunk. His body began convulsing in fast jerking movements.

Carolyn watched in horror as his head bashed repeatedly against the glazed concrete floor.

Tomas Grabbed Carolyn's hand and pulled her out of the room. As they passed the pantry, they could see Crandall thrashing and foaming at the mouth, the result of indulging in a few sips of Andrew's wine.

Together they shoved past the front door. The guard stood

confused, not trying to stop them. But by the time they'd reached the helicopter, the guard on duty had been alerted.

"Tomas! Behind you!" Carolyn screamed.

Tomas threw up his forearm as the guard charged at him. He blocked his sideways swing and pushed him. The man stumbled back. He was thick and awkward.

Tomas shook his head. Something wasn't right. His equilibrium was off.

The guard let out a deep grunt and ran at him. He tackled him shoulder to shoulder. He pushed, driving his feet into the ground until they reached the helicopter. The sturdy surface gave Tomas balance. He stepped forward and snapped out his fist. The quick jab shattered the guard's nose. The pain hadn't registered yet apparently, as the guard pivoted around and clipped Tomas in his flank. Only the glaring whites of his eyes were visible through his dripping, bloody face. The metallic form of a gun gleamed in his hand.

Tomas pulled the guard forward and punched him square in the bread basket—over his liver, beneath his sternum.

With his diaphragm paralyzed, the guard doubled over and gasped. The gun dropped to the ground and skittered off the side of the landing pad and pinged on rocks as it bounced down the hillside.

Tomas slipped to the left and yanked the man's head up by his hair. He positioned his right forearm tight around his neck. The guard's body squirmed and his fingers clawed at Tomas's arms trying to pull him off. Tomas continued to squeeze until the guard's struggle grew weak. His eyes bulged. Tomas grabbed the side of his head. In one swift motion he pushed it forward and then pulled back quick and hard until he heard the sharp crack.

Tomas looked back at Carolyn. Her eyes were wide with fear and her mouth gaped open. He gripped her hand and scrambled up the few steps into the helicopter. Instinct took over and he automatically clinched his seatbelt. The door wouldn't close. He banged it twice before reaching with both hands and yanked it hard.

He slapped at the starter button. His head shook, he stuck his tongue out, licked his lips, and then swallowed hard.

He squinted several times and stretched his eyelids open wide before lowering his face to the control panel.

"Tomas! Are you OK?" Carolyn shouted.

As the blades began to rotate, the air overhead pulsated. The increased frequency of the spinning rotor became higher in pitch with each passing cut. The compressor gauge stabilized and Tomas slowly cracked the throttle releasing fuel into the engine. The helicopter lifted in a rocky back-and-forth before climbing to the east over the dark sea. Tomas's head drooped, his eyes closed, and his chin drooped to his chest. Carolyn could see that he was straining to hold it up. He shook hard and when he regained himself, he immediately turned left toward mainland Tunisia. He leveled off at 200 feet.

"I've been a right door gunner and flight engineer," he said as Carolyn stared at him. His voice was calm but his face glistened with sweat.

"Tomas, you've been poisoned! "she said, fearing he'd collapse at any moment.

The radio crackled.

"I will kill you! I will kill you both!" Came the shaken voice of the double-crossed Ghet fah Mahryeed.

Just above three hundred feet, a searing white light shot up from the island. Exploding sound engulfed the helicopter.

Even with her eyes closed and ears covered, Carolyn felt the next blast.

Tomas screamed, "I can't see!"

The helicopter spun a half turn. Tomas jerked up on the collective stick and the bird went straight up, leaving their stomachs behind.

It hovered for a moment then began drifting downward. The blades sounded in a slap-slap vibration as they caught the wake vortex of too much power in a slow descent.

"My eyes! I can't see, Carolyn! How high are we?"

"Looks like two hundred feet! I'm not sure!"

Tomas took a deep breath and held his face close to the instrument panel. He adjusted a few controls and lowered the collective. The helicopter steadied its decent before climbing again.

He leaned his face on the window. His eyes drooped closed and his tongue dangled before he licked his lips.

"We've made 3,000 feet," he sighed.

They continued south as darkness closed around them. Carolyn's pulse had almost reached normal a short ten minutes later when they approached the desolate, pitch-black coast of the mainland. A slight sheen from the water delineated a rugged outline.

Thomas slowed the chopper and began his descent in a left, corkscrew pattern.

"Ugh!" he shouted as he turned a sharp left and then suddenly climbed in a tight spiral over a steep rocky outcrop.

"That came from nowhere!"

"Carolyn, I have to close my eyes for a few seconds. I need my night vision sharp to land. Please! Keep your eyes on the horizon!"

"I can't see anything Tomas!"

"Just keep looking!" he screamed.

After several moments, Tomas opened his eyes and looked at Carolyn. The light from the instrument panel bathed her face in a ghastly glow. He didn't say a word, but she knew he sensed her terror. She turned and closed her eyes.

The chopper bucked and swerved as Tomas fought the back wheels to the ground. He lifted his feet to engage the brakes. A large cylindrical object flew up from behind them. Tomas jerked the collective stick to pull pitch, but it was too late. The large tree branch hit the aft rotor on Carolyn's side. In that same instant a severe vibration shook the helicopter. The caution panel lit up and flashed the warning lights. They sparked and sizzled before going dark.

Tomas jerked both flight levers to a stop.

"Jump!" he yelled over the whirling blades and crashing tree limb.

Carolyn opened the door. She hesitated to step into the total darkness. The branch had flown clear but debris flew everywhere while the blades continued to idle. She looked back at Tomas.

"Jump!" he commanded.

In the reflection of his eyes Carolyn saw a brightness coming from behind him. As she turned to look back, Tomas shoved her out the open door. She reached, grasping at his arms as she flew out backwards.

The sudden thump on the rocks knocked the wind out of her. She curled in a ball, gasping for breath. Tiny missiles of sharp rock bit into her, scratching her hands and face. Still trying to catch her breath, she lowered her head and crawled back to the helicopter door. With the blades still circling overhead she was afraid she'd be hit if she moved away.

She could see Tomas struggling in the helicopter. She clutched the door and wiped the sand from her eyes. A blast of heat seared across her face and for the first time, she realized the light she'd seen behind Tomas was a flame. It had grown larger now and she could see that he was trapped.

"My seatbelt is stuck in the door. I can't get out!"

He pushed and pulled on the yellow striped handle just above his head. The jerking loosened the metal bolts until the handle sheared off in his hand. He whipped it aside, almost hitting her.

"Get back, Carolyn!" he screamed.

Tomas lifted himself in the tight cockpit area. He leaned, positioning his back on the control panel to get his legs free and kicked at the door. His high, loud grunts tore through the night, rising in pitch with each unsuccessful effort.

Carolyn's eyes streamed tears as she fumbled, reaching for something to break his window. In a flash of fire she spotted the windshield wiper. She balanced one foot on the door, holding only the window frame to stretch around to grab it.

A screeching crack came from behind. She pulled back from the windshield to a shower of hot hydraulic fluid. The tail rotor blew the oily fluid everywhere. Her eyes and skin burned as she coughed out the sugary-plastic slime and smoke.

Tomas pulled his knees back as far as he could and kicked. The door popped open. Across the open cockpit he could see Carolyn under the slowing blades clinging to the door. Her slick and sodden hair clung to her head and around her face. Her swollen eyelids squinted as she choked for breath.

"Run!" he screamed.

Tomas jumped. The blades overhead went from whop-whop to a crackling, grinding swoosh. They separated from the chopper, as if in slow motion, and flew out cutting into the air. The fire flared higher, blazing out of control as it reached the fuel tank. A cloud of noxious smoke spiraled as gallons of fuel shot into the turbine engine.

Carolyn had run almost twenty feet before the black smoke became a giant inferno roaring through the sky. The vibrations of the blast whip-slammed an instant pressure into her entire body. The shock wave hit her with a force so hard that it knocked her flat on her face.

It was just past midnight on December 25th, the day the son of man was supposed to have been born to save the world from its sins. Coincidentally, it was on that very night that Carolyn Wingate had committed the worse sin of her life. Murder.

A cold, plump dewdrop dangled precariously from the branch of a wind-bent Aleppo pine.

Plunk.

The drop hit her face. Her eyelids fluttered.

Trees of the Maghreb whispered in her ear, beckoning her attention. Her cheek felt cold. Yellow and orange flames twisted and turned, writhing through her dreams. She lay motionless, hypnotized by their dance. Suddenly her eyes flew open. Only red ash and smoke remained of the fire. With one eye she followed her frosted breath roll along the dirt.

She felt fuzzy. No thought. Gray.

She pulled to her knees, noticing that her fingers were numb. She was cold and her head hurt. Silvery bands of moonlight etched the spiny ridge-top a mile or so away. As her eyes grew accustomed to the night, she observed a dark, round form amidst the sharp and jagged landscape. She got to her feet trying to process what had happened. Still disoriented, she wondered about the lump. She walked toward it as she rubbed her hands together.

Even as she stood over him, her mind refused to accept that this was Tomas lying at her feet. She stood staring at him, eyes blank, mind empty.

The dim sound of helicopter blades grew louder and louder until she covered her ears. She searched through the dark sky. Nothing. The sound was in her brain. As it grew louder, she closed her eyes. The vision of Tomas screaming at her from an exploding flame jerked her to reality. She remembered.

All of it.

Andrew. Ghet fah Mahryeed. Tomas.

"Tomas!" she wailed.

But for the soft hum of wind and the muted breaking of faraway waves everything was eerily quiet. It caught her off guard. Weren't there spinning blades and a roaring blast just seconds ago? She knew there had been a blast, not because she remembered, because she hadn't. She knew because the last of the ash was floating to the ground like dirty flakes of snow and the smell of burnt engine fuel clung heavy in her nose.

She wondered how long she'd been out as she knelt beside Tomas.

"Tomas," she whispered as if trying to wake him from a nap.

No response.

"Tomas," she whispered again, this time reaching her hand around his neck to his throat. He was warm.

"Yes," she finally muttered as she felt a faint pulse.

A noise pulsated in the distance. She listened, wondering if it were real. Not waiting to find out, Carolyn reached under Tomas's armpits and dragged him behind a large ribbon of rock that created a fissure in the earth. A small boulder formed a natural stone turret. Gripping his body steadied her as she wobbled back and forth. Everything seemed gray. Her legs were rubber.

She broke a branch from the pine tree and scratched at the path Tomas's body made.

The noise grew louder. She knew they were coming.

Spotlights darted back and forth until they alighted upon the burnt helicopter. Its silhouette resembled the monstrous corpse of a giant spider. The embers of its hateful glowing eyes were hissing. Only the hulking body lay lifeless, crisp, and black.

The slender arms and legs must have blown away in the wind. Then Carolyn shook her head. There was no spider.

The lights swept out from the chopper searching the nearby area before suddenly making a sharp right turn and flying away toward Mahryeed's Island.

"Good! They think we're dead," she said to the still unconscious Tomas.

The wet, fuel-soaked dress sapped the heat from her body. Cold cut at her, scratching across her skin like frozen claws. She prickled with freezing pain as heat leached from her with each slow breath and rose in a puff of white vapor to dissipate into the night.

Carolyn struggled with stiff arms to lift the dress over her head. She tossed it aside and then slid her naked body between the rock and Tomas's silent form.

The heinous act she'd committed that night seemed years past.

CAROL GOODNIGHT

It may have only been a movie and not real at all.

The clammy chill that started in her hands reached deep into her body's core. She trembled violently as she shivered to generate body heat. She tried to think of firelight, saunas, and wine.

An hour passed as she listened for more searchers over the clattering of her shivering teeth.

At one point, a stray thought that she might already be dead entered her mind. And maybe Tomas, lying here next to her, was dead too.

She thought she should be afraid. But her fear floated out, away from her, just beyond her limp, numb hand that was stretched over Tomas's back.

After another hour, she was too tired to shiver.

I only want to sleep, she thought as she closed her eyes.

***

A light flickered over Carolyn's eyelids. She sensed heat warming the chill in her aching bones. She remembered the moon over the spiky ridge-top, the flaming chopper, and Andrew's bulging glare. She laid still, not wanting to open her eyes ever again.

But Tomas's urgent raspy groan roused her fully awake. The glare of the morning sun squinted her eyes almost closed again. The rock at her back was cold and the air still felt chilly. She realized the warmth she'd felt came from Tomas's fevered body.

Her knees were weak, and she felt dizzy as she struggled to her feet. Thickets of scrub and small evergreen trees surrounded them on three sides from the slopes of the Tell Atlas Mountains on this low coastal plain where they'd landed.

Sunlight dappled the hillside as it gently rose away from the rocks they'd used as shelter. As she searched the desolate landscape, a small gleam appeared through a thin fringe of trees. It looked like a tiny shack. A scattering of clouds drifted overhead and in the shade she lost sight of it. She stared at the spot trying to memorize its location. It lay just beyond a thick layer of dead brush.

Tomas groaned again. Carolyn knelt to feel his pulse. He felt hot. Hotter even than a minute ago. She rolled him to his side and unbuttoned his shirt. When she slipped it over his arms, she noticed the shiny divots in his back.

Gunshots, she thought. What monster would shoot a man in the back? She didn't wonder about it long. She already had a likely guess.

When she saw the long scar across his flank, her eyes widened. She followed the length of it with the tip of her finger wondering at the pain this man had suffered. She looked up to his face.

His thick black lashes fanned over his closed eyes. His peaceful expression looked as if he were taking a picnic snooze, not lying here near death at her hand. A sudden feeling came over her and she coughed as a tear rolled from her eye.

Tomas had been an honorable man. He'd been chivalrous and tried to save her in spite of her constant efforts at giving him the slip.

She should've trusted him. But how was she to know? Everyone man she'd ever known had let her down. Andrew especially. And Griff, of course. Even her brother left her alone and in danger when he'd died.

She knew he wasn't to blame, but…

Carolyn lowered her lips to caress Tomas's cheek.

"I'm sorry," she whispered.

With a new resolve, she stood up, slipped into Tomas's shirt, and then reached for her velvet gown. After laying it out smoothly next to him, she rolled Tomas onto it. She took a deep breath and wrapped her arms through the neck and armholes of the gown. A quick pull on the dress caused Tomas to roll to the side. The bullet in her arm ached.

CAROL GOODNIGHT

After repositioning him, she tugged at it, slow and steady, until she had him sliding along the loose rocks and sand. She lowered her head and dug her feet into the dirt, toes first, and pulled.

Tomas's breath became quick and shallow. His chest heaved in and out with short ragged gasps. Carolyn bent to check him. His pulse was weak and his skin had chilled. She carefully began pulling at the gown again with a renewed urgency. Sweat tickled her neck and rolled down her back. Her right arm was numb. White spots flashed under her closed eyelids, but she took a deep breath and kept moving.

Half an hour later she stopped to check their location.

When she turned back to Tomas, a thick scarlet trickle was dripping from his nose. It oozed down the side of his face into his ear. The garish red blood on his pallid skin gave him the look of a corpse.

Carolyn felt sick. Her knees buckled, and she fell next to him. She rested her face on his chest and listened to his heartbeat. It grew weaker.

A tear dripped onto his muscular shoulder and then dribbled down to his soft hairy chest.

And just like that, he stopped breathing. She lowered her face to his chest and listened.

Nothing.

The delicate beat of his heart had ceased. He'd slipped away. His final act of heroism was to end here on this bleak, windswept edge of the Barbary Coast.

"NO!" Carolyn screamed.

She'd poisoned this man. This hero. This defender of herself and this righteous revenge-seeker, even of her own brother's injustice.

Carolyn cradled his head in her palm and tilted it back to lift his chin. Her thumb and forefinger pinched together his perfect aquiline nostrils. She opened his mouth, placed her lips upon his, and began to breathe the whole of herself into him.

She gave him two breaths to see his chest rise before placing one hand over the other and pushing on his heart. Her mind went blank. Nothing mattered now. Only this. Only Tomas.

The sun had risen to mid-morning over the eastern set of hills. Too far from the ocean to hear waves, the only sound now was of the building Chichili winds blowing toward the Mediterranean and Carolyn's breathe breathing in and out of Tomas.

As she breathed harder and faster, a rush of noise roared through her ears and her skin began to feel clammy. As she pumped Tomas's heart, goose bumps ran up and down her arms. Little black dots swarmed in the outer portion of her vision before it became blurry and narrowed as if she were burrowing into a small tunnel. She lowered her lips to Tomas's as the hillside began to tilt at an angle and crash around her in a blur. She shared everything she had of herself with Tomas until she faded into black and collapsed over top of him.

They lay together in the field of dusty rock and scrub pine on that bright December morning while bug-eyed grasshoppers spit tobacco and bounced over them as if on trampolines.

A sudden blast of hot, dust-laden wind blowing from North Africa swept over the plain. The empty carcass of an emerald-green tiger beetle blew by them in a rush toward the coast. Low dark clouds followed helter-skelter like a mischief of rats upon hearing the rumor of bread.

Carolyn spun through the darkness. Round and round she tumbled. Her body frantically twirled and jerked as the wind rushing past her face made it impossible to breathe. She thought herself about to suffocate when the black murkiness leapt up to embrace her.

SPLASH!

She opened her eyes to find herself in a dank, dark hole. She floated.

Oh! The well!

Apparently time had skipped and she was back in Charleston. The idea seemed perfectly normal.

None of that had happened. Tomas wasn't dead. He hadn't even been there yet.

"It was a dream," she laughed.

The slimy wet walls of the well felt wonderful. She caressed the moss and smiled. She was home, in her dark place.

I'll never leave, she thought. *I'll sink, drown, and stay here forever. I'll let Tomas live. He'll take care of Andrew. I'm sure of it.*

She realized she'd grown to love this darkness. This lonely void.

She bent her head back and pushed off the wall. Contentment filled her. The answers were so clear now.

She looked up through the narrow opening of the well to the clear sky above. A sail drifted by.

That can't be, she thought. *It must be a cloud.*

She gasped a breath and looked closer.

It was a sail.

She clutched the side of the well and stared up at it.

A sail? In the sky?

A shadow covered the sky. When she looked again, she saw that it was Tomas. He was leaning inside the well with his hand outstretched toward her. His soft brown eyes, like those of a deer, were full of love and kindness as they beckoned her closer. A warm smile crossed his mouth. His lips were full and open.

His lips. His lips...

From somewhere outside the well, Carolyn heard a noise. She began to spiral again, floating upward this time.

"Nooo," she groaned.

She heard the noise again, this time in her ear. Carolyn

opened her eyes. The well was gone. Her dark place. Her comfort. Gone.

She looked up to find she was back on the rocky hillside. Back in the time when she'd poisoned Tomas.

Tomas coughed.

"Tomas!"

Carolyn jerked up.

I thought you were gone," she said.

She took hold of his strong shoulders and cried a flood of tears into the folds of his neck.

Tomas tried to say something but Carolyn continued to sob.

"Later," she mumbled.

Her arms were still around him as he lay there helpless. As she pulled away, she found her fingers lingering over his skin not wanting to let go. His precious life had been given back. After a while she wiped her face and scanned the hillside.

The sky had darkened and rain would be here soon. She stood up and reached into the neck of the dress again.

Tomas tried to move and say something.

"Later," she said and began to pull.

The small rock shelter was still quite a distance through the hilly, endless scrub.

Carolyn kept her eyes on the tall waving pine leaning over its roof like the gnarly tangle of a woodsman's beard as it whipped in the increasing wind. Churling grey clouds overhead made the world feel small and close. Only the two of them.

Air, already thick with the scent of upland conifers became thick with petrichor as the first fat drops pelted the brown earthen crust.

This wasn't the Sahara-like desert she'd expected when she'd thought about Tunisia. Which she had to admit, other than La Galite Island, she never remembered doing.

Funny, the things that run through your mind, she thought.

CAROL GOODNIGHT

Because of the approaching storm and the need to get Tomas sheltered, Carolyn headed straight up instead of taking to the left, a longer but less-vertical path. Her arms and back were numb now. The drop in temperature felt good on her soaking, sweaty body. She closed her eyes again and continued to pull. As it got steeper, she leaned forward, so as not to slip Tomas straight back down the incline.

It took a full five minutes to clear a path through the brambles while trying to keep an eye on Tomas's skin color and shallow breath. Finally, Carolyn dragged him through the wide open door of the abandoned shack and collapsed. She lay flat next to him, stretched out her back and groaned.

Thick, deep grooves from velvet digging into Carolyn's wrists and fingers made them slightly blue. She pulled her arms together and massaged them. A crust of dried blood covered her numb arm.

Rain came in a torrent. It battered the flat metal roof before soaking into the arid rocky soil outside. Carolyn turned her face toward the door. She felt woozy and her vision blurred slightly as she lifted her cheek from the dirt floor. A cloud of dust almost thick enough to conceal the sea rose from the parched earth as rain pummeled the hillside.

After regaining some strength, Carolyn sat up and scanned the small shack. It was a quick process with glimpses of the reality of their situation bleeding through until she was completely aware. Time hadn't existed in her haze of exhaustion. It was a weird sort of memory lapse where she wasn't where she last remembered being.

Where was that?

She looked down at Tomas. Half-way up the hillside he'd died.

She leaned down to kiss him. His eyelashes fluttered and she felt his breath brush her face as her lips lingered near his cheek.

She dragged Tomas the few feet to the short couch that sat against the back wall. Two worn and faded cushions propped in an attempt at décor did little to help the grim ambiance.

She set out a small clay bowl from the table under the overhang to catch the water draining from the roof. A moment later the bowl was full and she leaned next to Tomas to put the water to his lips. His eyes drifted open. He glanced around the room as he took a few sips.

Carolyn put her arm around his back and leaned him toward the couch. He rolled into it and closed his eyes again. Carolyn drank from the bowl and set it back to catch more rain. She crawled onto the slim couch behind Tomas and pulled the dress over them.

She lay in the darkness listening to the tree overhead groan in the furious roar and tumult of the wind. Large almond sized drops smashed against the thin metal roof threatening to pierce it like a bullet through soft flesh. Carolyn wrapped her arms around Tomas's back. His temperature seamed normal and his breathing was steady. She pulled him closer and molded herself to him as the cold bite of wind crept under the velvet gown. His dark-stubbled face lolled into the crook of her shoulder as his chest rose and fell against her. She began to breathe in unison with him and as their embrace generated warmth, her eyes slipped closed and she faded into black.

A sweet honey-like aroma wafted through the open door way to beckon Carolyn awake. Her stomach growled. She attempted to shift her arms and found herself unable to move. She opened her eyes to the angular curve of Tomas's strong jaw resting on her cheek. His arms were tight around her. A tiny dip in the middle of his plump rounded lips curved into an expression like that of a sinister angel. It was half smile… half sweet scowl. As he continued to sleep, he pulled her closer. She didn't want to wake him, but she needed to get away. She felt herself responding to his strong, warm embrace. He draped his leg overtop of her and murmured. She felt his manhood growing against her body.

She slowly pulled one arm from behind his back and then the

other. She pulled her hips back from his firmness and slid to the edge of the couch. With one foot dangling over the side, she slid over the edge to the floor. She closed her eyes and listened for his breathing. Satisfied that he was still sleeping she tiptoed to the door.

Sunrise sent shimmering rays of gold over the rocky hillside to the horizon of the placid ocean. She stood in the doorway and let the mango heat sink in, soothing her to the core.

Tomas is alive!

She lowered her head in relief. She hadn't killed him and this new day had brought a fresh page on which life could be written.

Hopefully Andrew was gone. As in dead! Carolyn was sure he couldn't survive that enormous gulp he'd taken.

With the thought of Andrew rudely guzzling wine, the corners of her mouth turned up a hint.

As the days went by, Tomas grew stronger. They ate from the olive and date trees surrounding the small hut. On the third day, Carolyn found a well in the weeds behind the hut and managed to pull up a few buckets of water. That night, however, she groaned in her sleep as she dreamed of the well in Charleston.

The experience of poisoning Andrew had dimmed her dark thing. In fact, she thought it was gone. But as she lay dreaming of the dark slimy walls, she felt it stirring. She groaned again.

Even though Carolyn protested, Tomas had been sleeping on the floor since the second day. When she groaned again, he slid into the cot next to her. He touched her arm gently.

"Are you Ok?" he whispered.

Carolyn woke suddenly, reached her arms around his neck began to sob.

"I'm so sorry, Tomas. For everything. I can't bear that you were hurt. It's all my fault," she cried.

"There, there," he said as he kissed her forehead.

"You are the bravest person I have ever known, Carolyn. Cuore mio," he whispered, "My heart."

Carolyn stopped crying and sniffed as she looked at him. He

stared at her and his eyes grew glassy with tear.

"I owe you my life," he said as he lowered his face to hers. Carolyn pulled him tight as her mouth hungrily nibbled over his stubbled face until she found the wetness of his lips.

He kneeled on the cot, pulled her beneath him, and gently caressed her shoulders as he peeled off his shirt she was wearing. The shirt tumbled to the dirt floor.

Tomas moved his hand over her cheekbones and kissed her with a raw, intoxicating intensity she'd never known.

In the silken light of dawn's twilight, they became one.

Early the next morning, the sound of choppers woke them.

"There's nowhere to run, Tesoro mio," Tomas whispered in her ear.

They clung to each other, ready for what came.

"Aliberti! Aliberti! AISE!"

"Tomas trembled as he held Carolyn in his arms and kissed her. When he pulled away he gasped, "We've been saved."

The chopper whisked them away to a private hospital in the Italian Alps. The staff did a cursory check on Carolyn and gave her release papers. They notified her there was a car waiting to take her home.

"I must see Tomas," she said.

"He is very ill ma'am. He has been poisoned," the nurse said.

"I must see him!" Carolyn demanded as she tore from the small room. As she rushed through the halls of the small clinic, she found a room with several doctors standing around a plastic-tented patient.

Carolyn held her breath and walked between them.

"You can't be here," one doctor said.

The nurse following Carolyn said, "She wants to say goodbye."

The doctors shook their heads and parted a path to the tent.

As Carolyn walked up to the bed, she could see Tomas convulsing.

"Tomas!" she screamed. "Tomas!"

The nurse gripped her arm and pulled her from the room.

"My dear, your hysterics will solve nothing. I have your information. You need to go home and rest. I will send word when Mr. Aliberti is ready to see visitors," she said. "But if I were you, I'd pray."

CHAPTER 15

The months passed with no word from Tomas although Carolyn had written him every week. She spent her days tending the vineyard, but the last few months she'd hired Ramone and Antonio to help.

She thought it was the least she could do. Tomas might need his home to recuperate. She'd keep it up until he returned.

As long as she would live, Carolyn would never forgive herself for hurting him.

As the tears slicked over her eyes, her heart caught at the memory of that one night with him. His gentle lips pressed against hers. How he held her. How he loved her.

For the first few months after she'd returned to the vineyard, Carolyn checked the newspapers and internet for any word about Andrew. After hearing nothing, and no sign from him, she finally began to relax. She reasoned that if Tomas needed months of care from his small sip of the poison, Andrew surely had died. And no one had cared enough to post anything about it.

One afternoon in late September, Carolyn heard Ombra bark twice and run toward the greeting bench in the front yard. She wiped her hands on her jeans and headed out the door to follow him. The grapes hung thick on vines between the gold and russet leaves and the hillside glowed amber in the glory of its autumn comforter.

"Not many customers these days. Huh, Ombra," Carolyn said. "Hope it's not that old Luca Benedetto tearing up the road again."

Carolyn sat petting Ombra's head as the car drove up and stopped. She couldn't believe her eyes when Griff stepped out.

"Griff!" she said. Her mouth gaped open as if to speak, but nothing else came. Her hands trembled as they scratched Ombra's head.

"Hi Carolyn," he said sheepishly.

Carolyn stared at him. A million thoughts ran through her mind.

"I'm sorry I never called you, Griff. So many things…" her words drifted off. She knew any excuse would be lame. She'd last seen him near Christmas.

"Listen Carolyn, I know I was a skunk. You don't owe me anything. But I just thought I owed it to you to tell you in person. You're a beautiful lady Carolyn. And I do love you. It's just that…" Griff halted. His eyes filled with tears as he held her shoulders.

Ombra pricked up his ears and barked twice before he charged off toward the house.

"Well, anyway," Griff said. "Julep is waiting for me in town. We thought we'd make this sort-of a second honeymoon. I'm so sorry Carolyn."

Carolyn closed her eyes for a long blink.

"There's something I want to say Griff," she said as she studied his face. The green in his eyes sparkled in that familiar way that always made her smile.

He truly does look happy.

"I wish you the very best, Griff. I truly want you to be happy."

Griff reached his arms around her and held her for a long time. Then without another word, he turned and rushed toward his rental car.

As Carolyn looked after him, she noticed a light flashing from the hill above the vineyard. At the same time, Ombra barked again from the house.

As Griff drove down the lane, a very expensive car waited for him to make the turn onto the main road. The driver, a dark man with a thick black mustache, glared at him. As he turned into the lane, Griff noticed the crisp white cuffs on his shirt when a shiny black cufflink caught the sun and almost blinded him.

"I hope he's a good customer, Griff said to himself. "I sure wouldn't want to deal with the likes him."

"Okay fella. I hear you. I'm coming." Carolyn called to Ombra as she took a last glance at the hill.

She could never have realized the light from the hill was Tomas walking home on his favorite path as he thought about his future now that he'd finally recovered. He'd stopped at the overlook, his favorite place on the vineyard, and pulled out his binoculars. His dark, serious eyes scanned the vineyard not able to bear another second without seeing Carolyn.

When he saw Griff embrace her, he sighed and hung his head. Without a second glance, he packed away his binoculars and turned to walk away. The cry of a lonely crow cut at him as he pulled out the small strip of blue velvet he'd kept from Carolyn's dress. He tossed it in the wind.

She also couldn't have known that Tomas had returned her yacht to the harbor filled with massive bouquets of red roses that were even now, faded and growing limp.

"I hear ya, fella," she said to Ombra as she walked into the room.

Ombra barked once more as Carolyn looked down into the cradle.

CAROL GOODNIGHT

"Hush, hush my darling. Momma is here."

The baby smiled up at her.

"You're such a beautiful boy," she whispered. "Every time I look at you, I see your father's eyes."

The End

A Note from Carol Goodnight

Thank you for reading Kiss of the Naked Lady. If you enjoyed it, please take a moment to leave a review at your favorite retailer such as Amazon USA. Please check out these other titles by Carol Goodnight.

amazon.com/author/carolgoodnight

BOOK 1 in the Carolyn Wingate Novella Series

A KISS IN DARKNESS

Broken-hearted from her CIA brother's accidental death, Carolyn Wingate, a successful Midwest construction executive, returns from his funeral to find that before his death he'd mailed her a lovely gold-and-diamond chain. Overcome with grief, she runs from everything she's known in a desperate search for solace.

Under the gentle swaying moss in the beguiling city of New Orleans she meets and falls in love with Andrew, a handsome, wealthy blue blood.

But a boat crash in the murky depths of a secluded bayou begins a string of perilous situations where Carolyn finds herself running again.

BOOK 2 in the Carolyn Wingate Novella Series

CAROL GOODNIGHT

THE KISS GOODNIGHT

On the run from her crazy ex, Carolyn Wingate finds the gentle waves and sunny shores of the Ligurian Coast of Italy a safe place to begin life again. A new yacht, new friends, and a funny new love almost let her forget the unhinged billionaire that can't seem to let go.

Almost…

BOOK 3 in the Carolyn Wingate Novella Series

KISS OF THE NAKED LADY

Two sublime seasons have passed and life for Carolyn Wingate couldn't be better. Griff follows her to the vineyard with a marriage proposal and a promise to love and care for her forever.

But the quick report of rifle fire and several bullet wounds set Carolyn on a new path…

A path of revenge.

A short story inspired by a character in A KISS IN DARKNESS

LADY CE'CIL

As Lady Ce'cil strokes the deep scar gashed through her forehead, over her eye, and across her cheek, she slips through time to the stagnate bayous and bald cypress hammocks of South Louisiana. It is in the sweltering summer of 1922 where she achieves fame in the hyperkinetic world of jazz in New Orleans at the sacrifice of love.

Like my Facebook page ~ Author Carol Goodnight

KISS OF THE NAKED LADY

Made in United States
North Haven, CT
29 May 2024